The Empress Irini Series

Betrothal & Betrayal
Poison Is A Woman's Weapon
Seizing Power
The Price of Eyes

By Janet McGiffin
Illustrated by Harry Pizzey

Book III

Seizing Power

Scotland Street Press

Published in 2024 by
Scotland Street Press
Edinburgh

All rights reserved
Copyright ©Janet McGiffin
Illustrations ©Harry Pizzey
The author's right to be identified as the author of this book
under the Copyright, Designs and Patents Act 1988 has been
asserted.

A CIP record for this book is available from the British Library.

ISBN: 978-1-910895-740

Typeset by Tommy Pearson
Printed on responsibly sourced paper
Cover image and design by Harry Pizzey

Many thanks to Jean, Paddy, Harry, Alex, Susan, Katerina, and Nellie.

EMPIRE OF THE RO

during the life of Irin

1. IKONION   6. PENDYKION
2. FILOMELION 7. NICOMEDIA
3. AMORION   8. HIERIA
4. DORYLAION 9. PROPONTIS SEA
5. NICAEA

AVARS

PAPAL
STATE

ROME

SLAVS

BU

THESSALONIKI

CALABRIA

LESB

SICILY

ATHENS

AEGEAN

CRETE

ROMAN S

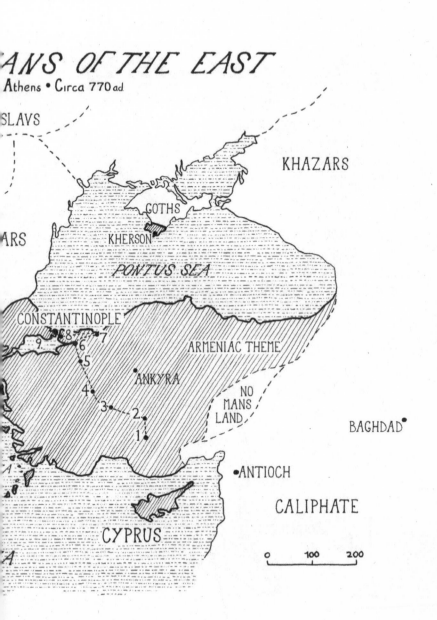

ANS OF THE EAST
Athens • Circa 770 ad

SLAVS

KHAZARS

ARS

GOTHS

KHERSON

PONTUS SEA

CONSTANTINOPLE
9   8   7
6

ARMENIAC THEME

5

4

ANKYRA

NO
MANS
LAND

3   2

1

BAGHDAD

•ANTIOCH

CALIPHATE

CYPRUS

0   100   200

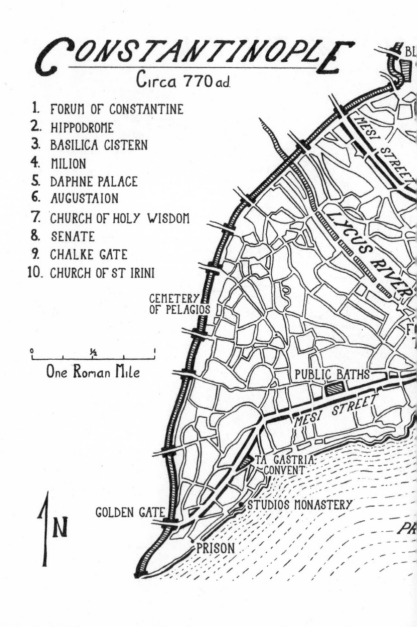

CONSTANTINOPLE

Circa 770 ad.

1. FORUM OF CONSTANTINE
2. HIPPODROME
3. BASILICA CISTERN
4. MILION
5. DAPHNE PALACE
6. AUGUSTAION
7. CHURCH OF HOLY WISDOM
8. SENATE
9. CHALKE GATE
10. CHURCH OF ST IRINI

CEMETERY
OF PELAGIOS

0 ½ 1
One Roman Mile

BL

MESI STREET

LYCUS RIVER

F

PUBLIC BATHS

MESI STREET

TA GASTRIA
CONVENT

STUDIOS MONASTERY

PR

N

GOLDEN GATE

PRISON

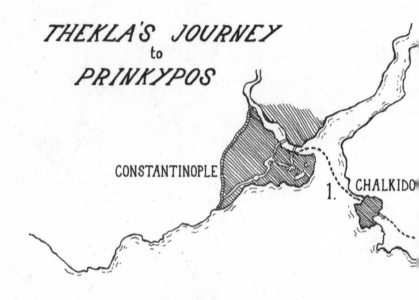

THEKLA'S JOURNEY
to
PRINKYPOS

CONSTANTINOPLE

CHALKIDO

PROPONTIS SEA

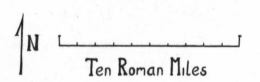

N

Ten Roman Miles

1. Ferry to Chalkidon
2. Twenty mile walk to Pendykion
3. Fishing boat to Prinkypos

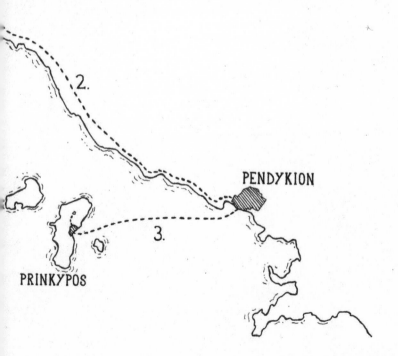

PENDYKION

PRINKYPOS

Chapter I

Aetios, the loathsome eunuch who was Empress Irini's chief guard, blocked me from entering the bronze doors of Empress Irini's chambers in Daphne Palace. The red tunica and black leggings that he proudly wore showed that he was a cut above the Palace eunuchs who wore white tunicas trimmed in purple.

"Step aside!" I snapped, and laid my hand on the knife in my belt. Aetios hesitated, knowing I would use it. Over his shoulder, I saw the eunuch Nikitas open the door.

"The Empress is in the map room, Abbess Thekla. Come this way," he called out cheerfully. Nikitas was a distant relative of the Empress. Once, he had told me with pride that his parents had made him a eunuch in infancy as a career move. Such eunuchs were docile and highly prized as house servants, as opposed to warlike eunuchs like Aetios who had been a soldier before Irini made him her personal guard. Nikitas led me down the passage and through the courtyard to Empress Irini's map room.

Empress Irini was with Stavrakios, the eunuch who was the Empress's second personal guard and as arrogant as Aetios. He and the Empress were talking to a short man with rounded shoulders whose tunica bore the insignia of an imperial jeweller. On a table between them sat a wooden box with the lid open. I glimpsed the top of a purple velvet crown with arched gold bands studded with jewels before Empress Irini and Stavrakios looked up at me and closed the lid. They returned their attention to the jeweller.

"Pearls," Irini said. "I want this crown covered with pearls. Everywhere you can sew pearls, sew them. My dear departed husband loved pearls."

The jeweller crossed himself. "Yes, Majesty. His Majesty had us sew pearls on all his clothing and shoes and . . ."

"I want the crown back here before dark."

"Of course, Majesty."

"Wear gloves," she added sharply. "I don't want dirty fingerprints."

"Certainly not, Empress!" He looked horrified.

Stavrakios locked the iron clasp and handed the key to the jeweller who fumbled it into a leather pouch on a cord around his neck. Irini waited until he had picked up the box, bowed awkwardly, and Stavrakios had led him out. Then she lifted the brocade curtain over the door to her bedchamber and motioned for me to follow. Her black silk ankle-length tunica swished against her loose black silk trousers. For once, she was not wearing jewellery; only her gold engagement ring gleamed as she sat down at her dressing table. She lifted a long pearl earring to her ear and gazed at her reflexion in a polished silver mirror.

"Why are you here?"

I was startled. "I came with Theo. To comfort Dino, I mean Emperor Constantine, like I did when his grandfather died." Dino had collapsed in sobs when Irini's cousin Theo had arrived in the imperial yacht with the sad news that Dino's father, Emperor Leon, had died. His grandfather had died four years before.

"Nine years old and he won't stop weeping," Empress Irini said critically.

"He feels overwhelmed." I also felt overwhelmed. The child whose birth I had witnessed in the Purple Room, who had taken his first steps into my arms, was now Emperor Constantine, Hand of God on Earth, Christ's Vice-Regent, Defender and Champion of the Faith, the sixth Constantine after the great one who built Constantinople. Only minutes ago, when we had stepped off the warship in the harbour of the Great Palace in Constantinople, the imperial guards had snapped to attention and dipped their spears. Palace eunuchs and officials wearing dark mourning clothes had crowded the steep steps to the Great Palace and dropped flat in full obeisance. Dino had clung to my hand.

"Dino must learn to control his emotions. Leon's funeral will be tomorrow, and Dino's coronation. The Senate will formally appoint me Regent."

I fumbled for words of condolence. "May the Lord help you in your sorrow."

"Don't be silly, Thekla. You and I have no need to

pretend. Leon never wanted me. His father arranged the marriage and all Leon could do was make my life miserable. The entire Palace is still whispering about how a month ago Leon stood right here and shouted that he would never enter my bed. That meant divorce and my exile to that convent on Lesbos where everyone dies. But Leon is dead and I'm still here. How mysterious are the ways of the Lord."

She lifted a string of emeralds to her throat and gazed in the mirror. "Only yesterday, my poor husband was kneeling in the Church of Holy Wisdom wearing that crown you just saw. Now he sleeps inside a shroud. I am having a memorial service in that same chapel tomorrow. The crown will be mounted on the wall—never to be used again."

I crossed myself. "How did he die?" I ventured. Theo had told me and Father Dimitrios, the village priest, when he came to the island to get Dino, but I couldn't believe it.

Empress Irini slid a large topaz ring on her finger and gazed at it. "His tuberculosis, the doctors said. It was getting worse. He coughed incessantly. He caught a chill during the ceremony and got his usual fever. This time, his doctors couldn't save him."

"What about the sores on his head?" I asked in a low voice.

Her eyes slid to me in the mirror. "Sores?"

"Theo said he had a ring of sores on his head where the crown had rested." Theo had also told us, weeping, that no ointment or salve could stop the pain of those boils and that he had watched his friend die screaming in agony.

"Leon did have some sort of rash. The tuberculosis, the doctors said. Poor Leon, gone to God in such a peculiar way. Which reminds me. . . Nikitas! Ioannis!"

The eunuchs appeared immediately. They must have been listening outside the brocade curtain. There were no secrets in Daphne Palace, the residence of the imperial family inside the walls of the Great Palace. Nor in any of the administrative palaces or workshops. Everyone gossiped, and the walls were riddled with peepholes. "Yes, Empress?"

"Go to my dear departed husband's closets and bring all his clothing with pearls or jewels sewn on it—shoes, hats, everything. And bring the rest of his jewels. They belong to Constantine now. Take Stavrakios with you, in case anyone gives you trouble."

I felt a growing sense of alarm. "Are those new eunuchs, Highness?"

"I had to replace the six eunuchs that Leon threw in prison, didn't I?"

"Are they still in prison?" Over the years, those eunuchs had become my friends.

"I told Stavrakios to release them and I would reinstate them as my household eunuchs. But Stavrakios said that a priest had forcibly tonsured them and the silly dears have taken their shaved heads seriously. They went off to be monks somewhere."

More likely, Stavrakios had threatened them and they fled, I thought. Stavrakios and Aetios cut off anyone who might get between them and Empress Irini. That included me.

"I will find them and bring them back."

"Don't. They want to be monks, so let them. You'll never find them in the hundreds of monasteries in Constantinople, anyway." She inserted a black pearl earring in her ear. "Why are you here?"

I was startled. "When Emperor Constantine died four years ago, you wanted me to stay with Dino while he viewed his grandfather's body. I thought you would want me to do the same for his father."

"No. Constantine is a big boy now. He will view the body with me today and tomorrow he will walk with me behind the Bier of Grief to Holy Apostles church for the entombment. I will be with him during the coronation, of course. It's not the real coronation, anyway; that will happen when he is eighteen. Tomorrow, the Senate will simply acclaim him Emperor and me as Regent for him. Go back to Prinkypos. You can still catch the ferry." She picked up a tiny glass vial of kohl and a tiny brush and began drawing black lines around her eyes.

I was speechless. Ten years before, when she was Princess, Irini had named me as Abbess of the Convent of the Theotokos that she sponsored on Prinkypos Island and told me that I was the only person she could trust. When she was with child, I had stayed with her in Daphne Palace because she had believed that her mother-in-law and sister-in-law were poisoning her and she wanted me to protect her. I had held her hand when Dino entered the world in the Purple Room of Daphne Palace. Dino's first word was my name; his first steps were into my arms. He had lived more in my island convent than in the Great Palace of Constantinople. Irini had made me vow loyalty to her and vow to protect her with my life. Why did she not want me to see my beloved Dino be crowned Emperor?

I found Dino sitting on his bed with his arms around Theo and his toy sheep which he hadn't touched for years. "Tomorrow I will be Emperor," he said, and his eyes filled with tears. "I will have to move into Papa's chambers. Grandpapa lived there before him. I wish Grandpapa was here. He would tell me what to do. You will come with me to see his body, won't you, Auntie Thekla?"

"I promise I will be near you." I put my arms around him and he fell asleep against my shoulder as children do when they are exhausted.

"You aren't staying tonight with Dino?" Theo frowned.

I looked away to hide the agony in my eyes. "She told me to go back to Prinkypos. But I will spend the night at Ta Gastria convent and watch the funeral procession with Abbess Pulkeria and her nuns, as I did when Emperor Constantine was entombed." When I first arrived in Constantinople from my village in faraway Anatolia, I had lived in Ta Gastria convent and worked as Abbess Pulkeria's accountant and scribe. Now that I was the Abbess of an imperial convent, Abbess Pulkeria treated me as an honoured guest and gave me a guest room. Theo started to say something, then flicked a glance at the doorway. Empress Irini was standing there.

"It's time to view the body," she snapped. "Wake Dino up."

Nikitas the eunuch stopped me as I was leaving her chambers. "I'll take you to the servant's passage in the

Hall of Nineteen Couches," he whispered. "You can view the physical remains from there."

I hesitated, suspicious of his motives. Irini might have sent him to spy on me and make sure that I left the Great Palace. Still, I had promised Dino that I would be near, so I followed Nikitas to the vast hall where banquets were held for hundreds of people. A stream of mourners were moving slowly by the bier where Emperor Leon lay in state. I caught a glimpse of purple robes and a simple band of gold crown across his brow. Empress Irini and Dino were looking down at him. She was dabbing her eyes with a black handkerchief. Dino was pale. Shadows smudged his eyes and his cheeks were wet. My gaze shifted to his father's five half-brothers standing behind Dino and fear struck my heart. The oldest two coveted the throne, urged on by their vengeful mother, ex-Empress Evdokia.

Across the hall, I spotted my mysterious friend and lover, Elias. A long time had passed since I had lain in his arms and I wondered when I would get my next opportunity. He had a room over the wheelwright in Pendykion, a seaside fortress across a narrow strip of the Propontis Sea from Prinkypos Island. He was postmaster at the postal way-station there and he came out frequently to the island to bring our mail. I always came down from the convent to see him. Every time we met, my arms longed to hold his muscular body. I missed our nights making love. But as an Abbess, I was supposed to be celibate. We could only meet alone when I came through Pendykion, returning from a trip to the Great Palace in Constantinople. In Pendykion, everyone thought I was his cousin. I would spend the night in his room and, in the morning, catch a ride to the island on a fishing boat. A long time had passed since I had lain in his arms but it wasn't by choice. It was lack of opportunity.

Today Elias looked pale and sad. His mourning clothes of gleaming black silk made his face look thin. The silk was a far cry from the disguise of a shabby monk that he wore when we had travelled together from my village in Anatolia to Constantinople eleven years before. Then, he had told me that he worked for the Eparch of the Monasteries, visiting monasteries to check that abbotts were not abusing monks with bad food or poor clothing. Since then, I had learned that he was not a monk, that he came from a rich Constantinople family, and kept a private room in a brothel where he met people who didn't want to be seen meeting him in public. His uncle had been a Patriarch, head of the Church, until Emperor Constantine had exiled him to Prinkypos Island and chopped off his head. Now Elias was the postmaster in Pendykion, a lowly position for a wealthy, educated man, I mused, as I had often done. I had slept in the man's arms countless times and I still didn't know who he really was. His gaze rested on me but not a flicker of recognition crossed his handsome face, as well it shouldn't. A wealthy man from Constantinople had no business knowing the Abbess of an island convent.

I left the Great Palace through Chalke Gate and nodded goodbye to the guards. I came often enough so they recognized me, even though I was wearing the undyed linen tunica of a nun and not the elegant silk or wool tunicas suited to the Abbess of an imperial convent that Empress Irini gave me to wear when I stayed at the Palace. I wondered again why she wanted me to leave before Dino was acclaimed Emperor. Pain stabbed my heart at the thought that she might keep Dino from me, now that he was Emperor Constantine.

As I passed the Milion, the low open structure where all roads in the Empire began, a hand dropped on my shoulder. My knife flew into my hand and I whirled to face my attacker. Then I smiled. "Elias, don't creep up on me! I might have slit your throat."

He took my arm, a surprise. Men did not touch women in public. "You look done in," he said gently, steering me towards a kapelarion. "Let's eat. How long are you staying at the Palace?"

"I'm not. I'm going to Ta Gastria convent. I'll go home after the coronation."

He raised his eyebrows. "The Empress doesn't want you to stay with Dino?"

I turned so he couldn't see my tears, but I know he saw them because he kept his hand tucked in my arm and sat me at a stone table outside an eatery near the Hippodrome. He ordered sausages wrapped in warm flatbread and a plate of mashed fava beans and grilled sardines. The September sun was warm and I drank half the pitcher of cool ginger and lime water, then devoured the juicy meat. I hadn't realised how hungry I was. The people sharing our table left and Elias spoke quietly. "Tell me about the crown."

I stopped chewing and looked at him cautiously. "What crown?"

He glanced around and lowered his voice. "Don't pretend you don't know. I'm talking about the crown that Leon wore in the ceremony the day before he died. People were whispering about it in the Hall of Nineteen Couches. They said that he had sores on his head where that crown was sitting. What did Empress Irini tell you? She trusts you; she must have told you something."

I returned to my grilled sardines. "Why do you want to know about the Empress? Are you spying for someone?"

He tore off a bit of flatbread, scooped up some fava paste, and ate it slowly, as if deciding what lie to tell me. "All you need to know is that next time when you find yourself in prison, I will get you out."

"You didn't the last time."

He put his hand on his heart. "Which I will regret to my dying day. You did get out without my help, I might point out. Just know that we are on the same side, you and I."

"Whose side is that?" I shovelled some flatbread and fava paste into my mouth.

"Our own side. We take a chance when it comes our way. We trust people only as far as we have trusted them in the past. We travel our own road."

I looked at his handsome face, his dark beard trimmed close, and his dark eyes gazing into mine, demanding information. I made my decision. Empress Irini was pushing me away and I didn't know why. I was afraid for Constantine and I needed a friend I could trust. Even though I didn't know who Elias really was, we had travelled together to Constantinople and had become friends—and lovers. I put my hand over my mouth so no one could read my lips, a trick I had learned from ten years staying in Irini's chambers in Daphne Palace.

"Where the crown sat on his head, his skin turned black. Boils. Deep sores. That's what Theo said. He was there when Emperor Leon died. The doctors used every ointment or salve they could think of, Theo said. Nothing stopped the pain. He died in agony."

Elias put a hand over his eyes. When he took it away, I could see tears. "Where is the crown now?" he asked hoarsely.

"Empress Irini is having the Palace jeweller cover it with pearls. She is holding a memorial in that same chapel tomorrow, after she is crowned as Regent for Constantine. The crown will be affixed to the wall, never to be worn again."

He took that in silence. "What caused the boils?"

"It was his tuberculosis, Empress Irini told me. That's what the doctors said."

He shook his head. "Tuberculosis doesn't cause sudden boils. What do you think?"

I spoke in a whisper. "It sounds like the Hellebore plant. If you touch the seeds, your fingers turn black and the skin peels off, with terrible pain. And if you then touch your mouth or eat it. . ."

"Hellebore. The most deadly of poisons." He drew a deep breath. "Did you mention your suspicions to the Empress?"

"I asked her about the sores. She said, 'What sores?' then said it was tuberculosis."

"Now you know why she doesn't want you in the Palace asking penetrating questions."

"Elias, surely she didn't. . . she couldn't. . ." I choked, unable to admit the possibility to myself. One month before, Emperor Leon had shouted at Irini that he would never again sleep in her bed. The Empress had rushed out to my convent on Prinkypos and locked herself in my study, terrified that the Emperor would have her divorced and exiled to the infamous convent prison on Lesbos. Now he was dead.

Elias took my hand, shocking me again. "Why don't you go on pilgrimage to some faraway shrine of some saint? Tomorrow I'll go with you to Chalkidon by ferry and put you on a coach." He spoke in a low, tight voice, unlike his usual breezy self.

"I can't, Elias. I'm an Abbess of a convent. My nuns need me. And Dino may want to come to Prinkypos and get away from this. . . prison. I promised that I will come to Constantinople whenever he sends for me."

His lips tightened. "If she lets him send for you. Tomorrow she will be named Regent which gives her complete power over Constantine until he is eighteen. And she is still Empress, even though Emperor Leon is dead. She has enormous power over the entire Empire." He put his elbows on the table and put his hands over his eyes. "Leon, my friend, all you got were four short years on the throne. You never had a chance to do what you wanted for the Empire."

We finished our meal in gloomy silence and he walked me to Ta Gastria convent, a long walk down Mesi Street over two steep hills. People had gathered in the Forum of Constantine and were speaking in low worried voices. Everyone looked sad. By the time we turned down the narrow steps to the Convent of Ta Gastria, dusk had crept into the small plateia in front of the open gate. Homeless women were lined up for a meal and a bed in the dormitory. Eleven years before, I had been one of those poor women needing a safe place to stay while I searched for my betrothed. Abbess Pulkeria had found work for me in the kitchen of Patrikia Constanta and I had stayed on at Ta Gastria as a paying boarder until I became Abbess Pulkeria's accountant and scribe. Today, I hoped that the Abbess had an available guest room for me. The wealthy convent was popular among rich women who came to Constantinople on pilgrimage to the Veil of the Virgin or other relics of saints sheltered in the hundreds of churches.

"When will I see you again?" I knew that he wouldn't say but I was delaying our parting. He often disappeared for long periods and never said where he had been.

"I don't know." He squeezed my hand and turned away.

The nun at the gate greeted me with a respectful nod. I stepped into the courtyard and relaxed into its familiar aromas of vegetable stew and incense from the little church. Abbess Pulkeria was standing at the door of her study as usual, her arms folded with her hands hidden in her wide sleeves and her eyes noting the face of each poor woman as she waited at the gate to enter. One shake of Abbess Pulkeria's head and the nun at the gate would turn the woman away. Troublemakers never got a second chance. Too many deserving women needed shelter.

I knelt and kissed the hem of her long tunica and she

placed her hand on my head in blessing. I took my place beside her, as I always did when I stayed there. I felt in awe of Abbess Pulkeria. She fed and sheltered hundreds of women, educated the poor girls of the neighbourhood, and ran a free hospice clinic for women and children.

"Good that you have come," she quietly gave the traditional greeting.

"Good to find you here," I replied in the traditional way.

"Empress Irini doesn't need you during this difficult time?"

"She told me to go back to Prinkypos. If you don't have a bed, I would be grateful for a space on the kitchen floor."

She nodded to the nun who closed the gate. More women were waiting outside but the dormitory was full and food was cooked only for a certain number. Ta Gastria was an imperial convent and Abbess Pulkeria had to account for the stipend she received from the Treasury. She also got donations from wealthy families and she charged a hefty price for her guest rooms.

Abbess Pulkeria motioned me into her study where she poured out two tiny glasses of elderberry wine. We sat on the couch by the window so she could keep an eye on the women entering the kitchen holding their bowls and spoons. "Tell me about this crown that Emperor Leon wore at that ceremony."

"How did you know about the crown?" I stammered.

"There are no secrets in Constantinople. Were there actual boils where the crown rested?"

I nodded. "Empress Irini's cousin Theo told me. He

was with Emperor Leon when he died. In terrible pain, he said."

"Did Empress Irini tell you anything?"

"The doctors said the boils were tuberculosis, she said."

Abbess Pulkeria refilled our glasses soberly. "I have seen a lot of tuberculosis and I have never seen boils. Two emperors have died since Irini of Athens arrived in Constantinople—two healthy males dead in four years. Now we have a nine-year-old Emperor controlled by her. One day, we will learn the truth." She then spoke briskly. "I can only offer you this couch for the night. The guest rooms are full. Women are here for the entombment and coronation. And there is no room in the dormitory."

"I am grateful for whatever you can spare."

"You will eat in the private dining room."

"I prefer the refectory with the poor women, if you don't mind." I didn't want to face the curiosity of rich women.

I went to the church for evening prayers. After eating lentil stew with carrots and leeks, I spread a quilt on a couch in the study. As tired as I was, I lay thinking for a long time. Emperor Leon had died screaming in agony. Was it really hellebore poisoning? Would we ever learn the truth?

The next day, I watched the funeral procession from the terrace of a convent that overlooked Mesi Street. Four years before, from this same terrace, I had watched the body of Emperor Constantine pass by in the Bier of Grief drawn by four white horses, his face open to the sky. Behind him had walked his son Leon with Irini, Dino,

Leon's five half-brothers, and mournful bishops, priests, soldiers in dress uniform, patricians, and diplomats. Today, as then, they were taking our Emperor to the Church of Holy Apostles where he would be sealed inside a tomb near his father, grandfather, and all the emperors before them, back to Constantine the Great. I did not weep for Emperor Leon as I had wept for his father. Leon had never ridden through the streets with his hand held up to bless us, as had Emperor Constantine. I had never felt as protected by Emperor Leon as I had by his father. I hoped that Dino would become the emperor that his grandfather had been.

The next day, I didn't see Dino be acclaimed Emperor, nor Irini be named Regent because the guards wouldn't let me into the Church of Holy Wisdom and I had no letter from Irini to make them. So I caught the ferry across the Propontis Sea to Chalkidon and sat on deck gazing into the blue sea and clear sky. Abbess Pulkeria was wrong. There were secrets in Constantinople. Two emperors had died abruptly. And no-one knew that Elias and I were lovers except for one person and she would never tell.

I spent the night in a convent in Chalkidon and dined on Saint's Broth—water, onions, herbs, and a few drops of oil poured over dry bread. My stomach grumbled with hunger all night. In the morning I bought cheese, bread, and olives which kept my stomach happy for the twenty miles to Pendykion. Elias was there already, boosting a mail courier up on his horse when I came through the passage through the high walls. We had supper at the kapelarion by the inn. We spoke little. I could feel his sadness and anger. And something else.

"What are you worried about?" I asked later, as I lay in his arms in his room over the wheelwright. My stomach was full and my heart content.

"I worry about the boy." He tightened his arms around me and I fell asleep.

In the morning, he took me in his mail boat to Prinkypos.

Chapter II

Only weeks after the entombment of Emperor Leon, Empress Irini sent imperial messengers across the Empire announcing that she, as Regent, would be giving out the annual salaries to the high-level imperial employees. That included army commanders, governors and administrators of the themes, and upper-level employees in the Great Palace. And me, as administrator of an imperial convent. Elias delivered the official letter: I was to appear at the Great Palace the last week in October to accept into my hands a purse containing the stipend for the convent. From that I had to pay each nun and novice her stipend, cover our expenses such as the stonemason and carpenter for repairs to the convent, pay Father Dimitrios to hear our confessions and give communion once a month, and buy our fish from the local fishermen. If there was any left, it went into my purse for my old age.

So, forty days after the lid of the sarcophagus had scraped over Emperor Leon, Sister Matrona and I stood on the quay with Father Dimitrios waiting for Elias to come in his mail boat to take me to Pendykion. I would take the mail coach to Chalkidon, then board the ferry to cross the Propontis Sea to Constantinople.

I was eager to go but at the same time, I hated to leave the island. The stifling heat of summer was only a memory and we slept more deeply and ate with more satisfaction in the cool. The trees were turning autumn gold and red, the grapes were heavy on the vine behind every village house, the branches of the olive trees hung low with fruit. The scent of new-mown barley drifted from the fields that climbed the hill from the village up to the convent. Our chickens were laying more eggs and the nuns went about their chores with a lighter step.

Our days revolved around our three prayer services. We woke at dawn to the bang of Father Dimitrios's semantron that floated up the hill from the village and filed sleepy-footed into the little church in the courtyard for Orthros prayers. Then we filed into the refectory for porridge, fresh cheese and fruit which Aspasia had ready for the novices to hurry to the table. We chatted at table, unlike some convents that demanded silence.

Chores kept us busy until the next meal. Some nuns and novices fed and milked the goats and sheep, shooed them out to pasture, and tended the garden, grape arbour, and orchard. Others swept the rooms and courtyard, cleaned the latrines, then sat at the looms or copied scrolls. Sister Evanthia and Sister Filothei taught the village girls their letters and Sister Efthia cared for patients in the hospice.

Our mid-day meal was our largest and came after Ninth Hour prayers. Aspasia cooked vegetables, lentils or beans, eggs, fish, mussels or other seafood, and the occasional chicken. Some monasteries only ate creatures that did not bleed, but our hard labour demanded meat or we became weak. We drank fresh goat milk or kitron juice sweetened with our honey. In summer we rested in the heat of the day, then returned to work until prayers at dusk and a light meal of cheese, flatbread, olives, and watered wine. In winter, we drank more wine and herbal tea to keep warm.

Larger convents held prayer services through the dark hours and had nuns who only prayed and led the services. Their nuns were isolated from the outside world. But we were too small to divide the labour, and the nuns got irritable when we only had each other to look at. So I took them down to the village to join the religious feasts and they joined me when I bought fish or helped Sister Efthia visit the sick. We lived a harmonious and full life and Sister Matrona's stern eye made sure that everyone did their share.

There was just one problem. Megalo.

The evening before, Sister Matrona, my second-in-command as ekonomis, had come to my study with Sister Efthia, Sister Evanthia, Sister Filothei, and Aspasia. They had stood before my desk and demanded that I expel one of our novices, fifteen-year-old Megalo. Her husband, Fanis, had joined a monastery and, instead of giving her a divorce, had ordered her to become a nun. Megalo had been an attendant for Empress Irini and had often come to Prinkypos with her, so Megalo had asked to join our convent. Empress Irini told me to accept her on probation. I did so but as a resident, not a novice. I knew Megalo. She was a sweet and spoiled girl from a rich family who didn't know the meaning of work. Our typikon, our founding documents, read that women must take the vows by their own choice, not by a husband's order and Megalo was hardly there by choice. No one was happy. Megalo's mother, Patrikia Constanta, wanted Megalo to divorce Fanis and re-marry, the nuns were annoyed by Megalo's lazy habits, and Megalo was bored and lonely for city life.

"Megalo mopes around like living here is punishment, not her choice," Sister Matrona accused in her powerful voice that could carry through a fog bank. I always felt small next to her, despite my height. And humbled, when I watched her strong arms pull out a lamb stuck in the birth canal and her gentle hands pump air into its lungs.

Sister Filothei added in her sweet soft voice that somehow kept the village girls quiet in her class. "She is terrified of goats, sheep, chickens—indeed any of God's creatures. She is so afraid of the dark that someone has to hold her hand when we go up to bed!"

Sister Evanthia's normally calm voice trembled with agitation. "She has only the four smallest girls to teach their letters and their screaming disrupts the entire convent. And they cannot read!"

"She faints at the sight of blood or pus," said Sister Efthia. "She cannot even hold the dressings when I am cleaning a wound."

"Get her out of my kitchen," Aspasia demanded forcefully in her deep voice. "She scorches the porridge. She threw up when I made her gut the fish."

I grimaced. Their complaints were not new. "I am marking the days until her six-month probation is over and I can send her home."

"Send her now," said Aspasia flatly. The nuns nodded vigorously.

"Have you given Megalo the letters she is getting?" Sister Matrona demanded. Her sharp eyes took in everything, as they should. The ekonomis directed the convent whenever I was summoned by Empress Irini to Constantinople.

"If I had, Megalo would be more melancholy than she is now. See for yourselves." I drew a bundle of letters from my desk drawer. "These are from her mother and from Tisti, another of Empress Irini's former attendants, and from Tisti's son, Theodore. None from her husband, Fanis-The-Wife-Abandoner."

Sister Matrona scanned one of the letters and made a face. "Patrikia Constanta only writes about her parties. Give these to Megalo to remind her of her rich life. She will go home."

Sister Efthia frowned as she read. "Theodore writes how happy Fanis is being a monk. It's time Megalo stopped this nonsense of taking the vows because that horrid man wants it. Empress Irini will grant her a divorce. She won't refuse, like Emperor Leon did, weak man that he was."

Sister Matrona was reading another letter. "Theodore writes that Brother Fanis is planning to build his own monastery."

"No doubt he is using Megalo's dowry to build it," I said, grimly. "Brother Fanis has little money. Emperor

Constantine supported him and his mother after his father died. He and his mother moved into Megalo's parents' house when he married Megalo. He had a Palace salary but that went when he took the vows and moved into a monastery."

I had taken a dislike to both Fanis and Theodore the day I met them in Princess Irini's reception ten years before. They had been ten years old then, the sons of two of Irini's attendants, and they spent their time in the Princess's reception happily arguing over scripture and the writings of the Holy Fathers. Fanis couldn't be bothered even to speak to Megalo, who was already his betrothed. They were to be married at age fourteen.

Aspasia tossed the letters back on my desk. "Send Megalo home soon or she will be too old to find a husband."

I winced. I myself had been an old bride of seventeen when my betrothed, a soldier, had left me waiting at the church for the third time. Desperate to wed before my father sent me to a convent, I had chased my betrothed to Constantinople. Irini, who had been Princess Irini then, had tracked him down and forced him to release me from my betrothal contract. She had persuaded Emperor Constantine to name me as Abbess of the convent she wanted to sponsor on Prinkypos. She didn't care that I had never taken the vows of a nun; she only wanted a refuge to escape the Palace whispers and malicious gossip. She said that I was the only person she could trust. I had to trust her, in return. She knew that I had lied to Emperor Constantine that I was a nun. Others had guessed the truth—Elias, for one. Sister Matrona knew, because she and I had lived at Saint Emmelia where I claimed to have taken my vows. Aspasia told me that she didn't think I was a nun, but she didn't care. I drew a breath.

"When I go into Constantinople tomorrow, I will tell Patrikia Constanta to come and get Megalo. Send her in and I will give her the news."

Megalo came in rubbing her chapped hands with a bit of sheep wool. "Isn't it funny how you used to be a servant in our kitchen and now I am working in your kitchen?" she asked in her innocent way that never failed to annoy me.

"Your mother stepped on my hand when I was scrubbing the flagstones," I snapped, making clear how different my work had been from hers. I folded my hands on my desk. "I called you here to discuss your desire to join this convent as a nun, Megalo."

"Please call me Sister," Megalo said in her shy little voice.

"You aren't a nun," I snapped. "Just because your husband told you to take the vows doesn't make you suited for a life serving God."

Tears filled Megalo's wide eyes, causing me a twinge of conscience. Who was I to tell this girl how to serve God when I myself had never taken the vows? Truth be told, the lie hadn't bothered me until after both Emperor Constantine and Emperor Leon had died. That was when I began to feel uncomfortable being the head of a community of women who believed that I was what I was not. I kept telling my conscience that keeping these women safe and content was my way of taking the vows. Indeed, chanting the daily prayers of Orthros, Ninth Hour and Esperinos did replenish my lagging spirits and give me strength. But still came that small voice of conscience.

Megalo stuck out her lower lip in a pout as she had done often when I was a servant in her house and had to coax her out of bed. "I am trying, Thekla. I mean Abbess Thekla."

The pout hardened my heart. "You sleep through the bang of Father Dimitrios's semantron at dawn in the village so you are late for morning prayers. This is when our day begins. The rituals of a community must be followed or communal life breaks down."

A whine entered Megalo's voice. "I get tired working in the kitchen. And teaching the little girls wears me out. Can't you give me something easier? When I was an attendant for Princess Irini, we just sat and waited for her to want something."

My limited supply of patience ran out. "You have four little girls to teach for two hours a day. Their screaming disturbs us all. I asked them to read a few words. They cannot. Your cooking is abominable. You are still afraid of goats. This is not the convent for you."

Megalo collapsed into sobs. "Please give me another chance, Thekla. I mean Abbess. Fanis will be angry with me."

That finished it. My voice went hard. "A husband gives his wife children. Or tries to. Empress Irini will get your marriage annulled and your mother will find you a proper husband. I am going into Constantinople tomorrow. I will tell your mother to come and get you."

I handed over her letters. "These came for you. Sit over by the window and read them so you know what you are going back to."

"The seals are broken!" Megalo gasped.

"Abbesses read nuns' letters. To help with what is troubling them."

I watched her lips move slowly as she read. No wonder she couldn't teach the little girls; she could hardly read, herself. She looked at me mournfully.

"Theodore writes that Fanis has taken the vows at Polychronos Monastery. Fanis writes to Theodore but he doesn't write to me!"

"Divorce him," I snapped. "Marry a real man."

The next morning, I smiled as I waited on the quay with Father Dimitrios and Sister Matrona watching Elias steer his little mail boat into the tiny harbour. "I will soon see Dino," I said happily. "I will accept our yearly stipend. I will tell Patrikia Constanta to take Megalo home. I will eat grilled shrimp at my favourite eatery by the Hippodrome, I will stay the night at Ta Gastria, and come home."

Sister Matrona tightened her lips. "Dreams of the future are self-indulgence masked as planning. Do not look too far ahead."

She was right, because when Elias docked, our future changed. A little monk wearing a long worn sheepskin coat and a brown leather cap with ear flaps climbed stiffly out. He was dragging a large leather bag that looked as worn and tired as the monk himself.

"Welcome, Brother!" Father Dimitrios called out warmly, taking the monk's bag and clasping his hand.

"What has brought you our way?"

The monk pointed at Saint Nikolaos church and started walking there. Father Dimitrios looked at Elias, who shrugged.

"He was waiting at the harbour and he showed me a letter addressed to Abbess Thekla. He hasn't spoken a word."

We followed the little monk into the church. His lips moved when he prayed but he made no sound. I glanced at Elias and Sister Matrona, who looked puzzled. Father Dimitrios invited us into his cottage. The little monk remained silent as we sipped our mountain tea and ate the warm flatbread that Father Dimitrios's wife had cooked on the curved iron plate over the hearth fire. Their latest baby lay sleeping in the cradle by the fire. Village priests were expected to marry and have children. Monks and bishops were celibate, or supposed to be.

The little monk made the sign of the cross over his bread and nibbled at it in silence. I identified myself and he promptly drew a rolled up papyrus from his shabby bag and handed it over. I cracked the red wax embedded with Empress Irini's seal and read aloud.

"'The bearer of this letter is Brother Grigorios, iconographer. I am paying him to cover your convent church with icons—walls, ceiling, pillars. Brother Grigorios trained at Pelekitis Monastery in Bithynia until Mihalis the Dragon burnt it down. He fled to Antioch in the Caliphate and then to the Holy Land. He recently returned to Constantinople with Brother Yiorgios, my tutor in history. Father Dimitrios will find lodging and meals for him.'"

Father Dimitrios was gazing at the monk with awe. "Thanks be to God that you have reached home safely, Brother Grigorios."

The monk nodded and crossed himself. Elias frowned.

"Brother Grigorios, we are not in the Caliphate where the Caliph lets you paint icons with impunity. Here in the Empire, icons are still banned by edict. Empress Irini can pay you to paint icons because she is Regent for our young Emperor. He is only nine and we do not know how he will regard icons when he is eighteen and takes the throne. However, there are many bishops and army officers who would gladly enforce the ban on icons and they could cause you a great deal of suffering—even death. The Empress may not be able to save you."

Brother Grigorios nodded and watched us with his intense gaze.

Father Dimitrios broke the silence. "Do you understand that you may suffer exile or death for your holy labours, Brother?"

The monk nodded and pointed upwards.

"May God keep you safe," sighed Father Dimitrios. "And us," he added, crossing himself. A smile then brightened his bearded face. "Now, Brother, tell us of Bethlehem! And Jerusalem! Have you seen where Our Lord was born? Have you seen the stone that they rolled away from the tomb? Tell us!"

The monk smiled sadly. He pulled off his cap. Where his ears had been were only holes. He opened his mouth. There was no tongue, just a red stump. Sister Matrona and I gasped in horror. The monk put his cap back on and continued to watch us with his bright eyes.

Father Dimitrios drew a breath. "We will find you lodgings. Until then, you will live in the guard's cottage where they stay when the Empress is in residence. The village women will bring your meals."

The monk looked at me and raised his eyebrows. I found my voice. "Sister Matrona is my ekonomis. When you are rested, come up to the convent and she will show you our church where you will be working. I am going to Constantinople now, but I will be back in a few days. We can discuss your work then."

Elias handed Sister Matrona three letters for Megalo, then he and I climbed into the mail boat. As soon as he had rowed out of the little harbour and had raised the sail, he turned to me.

"Bad news. I couldn't speak of this in front of the others. Empress Irini has arrested Constantine's two oldest uncles, Nikiforos and Christoforos. She has accused them of plotting to seize the throne."

My jaw dropped in dismay. "Surely not—they are too young to have followers who would dare such a thing."

He shrugged. "No one knows anything about it. She has stripped them of their titles of kaisar and had them tonsured as monks. They're locked inside a prison monastery on the other side of the Bosporus Strait. As if this weren't enough, she called the senators and patricians to a meeting. She announced that on the Day of Nativity, Patriarch Pavlos will guide the two brothers through giving the Eucharist in the Church of Holy Wisdom. Once a monk has said the divine liturgy, he is a priest. A priest can never be an emperor."

I felt ill. "Just the two of them in this conspiracy?"

He shook his head. "The Empress has also arrested three highly respected, high-ranking army officers and several members of the Palace Guard who were appointed by Emperor Leon. All were tonsured and exiled. The postal couriers told me that people are gathering outside Chalke Gate and shouting that they want a different Regent for Constantine. Empress Irini has sacrificed high-ranking officers with battle experience just to get rid of Constantine's uncles. This, the army will not forget."

He adjusted the sail to catch the wind. "Empress Irini is planning to announce her new appointments for military commands and administration after she hands out the salaries. As Regent, she can name new staff. But she would be wise to wait a year and learn from those who hold those positions. They gave good counsel to Constantine's father and grandfather. He needs to learn from them. Point that out to her."

I shook my head. "She won't listen to me. She is taking her revenge."

Chapter III

Elias put me on the next coach to Chalkidon but it was slow and I missed the last ferry to Constantinople. I spent the night in a convent and caught the morning ferry feeling tired, needing a bath, and desperate to see my beloved Dino. I had to force my way through an angry crowd outside Chalke Gate shouting that they wanted Nikiforos and Christoforos freed. The soldiers at the gate recognised me and they pulled me inside, but they were under instructions to get permission for anyone to enter, so I had to wait while they sent a messenger to Empress Irini.

Theo came to fetch me. I liked Theo. He adored Dino and whenever he brought Dino to Prinkypos for a day's excursion, he sat on the bench by the church with Father Dimitrios and me to chat. He loved Irini, anyone could see that. I had watched him try to shield her from the cruel jibes of Empress Evdokia and her cronies. But Theo had also been a close friend of Emperor Leon and I wondered if Leon's death would change Theo.

"I want you to speak to Irini about a few things," he murmured as we walked slowly toward Daphne Palace. He put his hand over his mouth to hide his words from the people around us.

"Why don't you talk to her?" I forced my steps to slow to his, frustrated at the delay in seeing Dino.

"She doesn't listen to me," he said with some bitterness.

"She doesn't listen to me, either. I don't even know if she will allow me to stay with him. She ordered me to leave before the funeral and coronation. I may have to stay at Ta Gastria."

He sighed. "Irini thought that Dino would not control his emotions at the entombment if you were there, that he would be wailing and sobbing. She kept him beside her every minute through the funeral and coronation."

When I said nothing, he went on. "After Irini hands out the salaries in the ceremony, she will announce her new appointments to high-level administrative and army positions." His lips tightened. "She is being damned secretive about it. She won't tell me the names but I have my suspicions and they aren't good. She should wait at least a year and gain the experience of the people who hold those positions. They will train Constantine in administration and give him good advice."

Elias had said the same, in nearly the same words. I wondered how well they knew each other. "Did you tell this to Irini?"

He nodded, gloomy. "She told me that she was Empress and I should keep my opinions to myself." He gazed at a wren chattering at us from a bush. "The truth is, I would happily go home to Athens. I only stay because Constantine needs a father and I'm all he has. Talk to her, Abbess Thekla. Tell her to wait a year before she names new appointments."

I shook my head. "She will get angry and she might keep me from seeing Dino."

He lowered his voice. "Irini is walking a dangerous path by arresting Dino's uncles—trouble for herself and for Constantine. The army could decide that she is not a suitable regent and rise against her. They will install some commander as regent who could decide he wants to wear the crown. We could have a Palace takeover. I cannot guarantee Constantine's life."

His words horrified me. "I will speak to her," I promised when I found my voice.

A stream of visitors crowded the marble steps of Daphne Palace. Theo stopped me. "Another problem: Consul Elpidios is back from Sicily. It isn't wise for her to see him alone. He is married and Irini is supposed to be a grieving widow. Talk to her."

"Theo, she won't listen to me. I keep telling you."

"Try. Go to her reception hall so she knows you are here. Besides, she will want you to see her last two visitors."

Empress Irini was lounging on a cushioned couch atop the dais at the end of the long hall where Empress Evdokia used to entertain her dozens of attendants. Now it was empty except for former Empress Evdokia and her daughter, Anthusa, who were standing before Irini. A scribe sat at a table to the side with stacks of papyrus, parchments, and bottles of ink. Aetios stood guard.

Evdokia was leaning on a cane. She had shrunk since I had seen her four years before, when Irini became Empress as wife of Emperor Leon and kicked both Evdokia and Anthusa out of the Palace with only the clothes on their backs. They had moved into a small convent across Constantinople. I had gone with Irini to visit them and Evdokia had complained about their lack of warm clothes and comfortable bedding. Now I was taken aback at how thin Evdokia had become. Her faded red tunica hung on her. Her face had narrowed and I could see traces of the beautiful woman that Emperor Constantine had taken as his third wife. Anthusa wore a dull nun's habit and rough sandals. A large wooden cross hung on a leather strap around her neck.

Empress Irini was smirking with pure satisfaction. "Anthusa, dear, doesn't your convent provide you with decent clothing?"

"You summoned us here, Irini," Anthusa said evenly. "Tell us what you want."

"I want your assistance—yours, not your mother's. I am inviting you to be my Co-regent. To help me advise my son. In your strangely devout way, you can present him with a different point of view."

Anthusa burst out laughing. "Co-regent? Irini, dear, let us not pretend your offer is serious."

"My son might need counsel from a religious person. I can't imagine why, but it might happen."

"Let Patriarch Pavlos advise him. He will say what you want; I will not. Anyway, Constantine doesn't need my advice. He is an intelligent boy and he will learn what he needs from his advisors."

"Then you are refusing my request to be Co-regent?" Irini smiled.

"Definitely. I will absolutely not accept the position of Co-regent."

Empress Irini turned her head a fraction toward the scribe. "Let it be written that Princess Anthusa, paternal aunt of Emperor Constantine, refuses Regent Irini's request to be Co-regent."

Her gaze moved to Evdokia. "You are communicating with your two oldest sons after I warned you not to contact them. They are locked in a monastery to keep them out of mischief while they await their punishment on the Day of Nativity. At that time, they will be brought to the Church of Holy Wisdom where, in front of everyone, Constantine will tonsure them and ordain them, guided by Patriarch Pavlos. Then the Patriarch will guide your sons through the celebration of the Eucharist. Once they have given the Eucharist, they are priests. A priest cannot be emperor."

My heart sank. I had hoped that Irini had changed her mind about the punishment.

Former Empress Evdokia's face twisted in anger. "My sons have done nothing against you. You made up this conspiracy whole cloth. You always were a liar."

Empress Irini's voice remained smooth. "Be careful, Evdokia. I could confiscate whatever money you have left and exile you to that convent on Lesbos where everyone dies. The poet Sappho died on Lesbos. Her ghost will keep you company."

Cruel words, but I felt no pity for either Evdokia or Anthusa. Fresh in my memory were the ten years I had watched them snub and ridicule Irini. They had spread rumours that she was praying before icons hidden in her closet, and that she had committed the treason of having unlawful relations with her cousin Theo, with Elpidios—and even with her private physician, Doctor Moses.

Evdokia flushed with fury and pointed a shaking finger at Irini. "Shame on you! What would Emperor Constantine think of you now? What would your husband think?"

Empress Irini smiled. "Emperor Constantine told me that I reminded him of his first wife, and that he had loved her to his dying day. As for Leon, I didn't care what he thought when he was alive; why would I care now?"

She dismissed them with a flick of her fingers and motioned for me to follow her into her map room. Stavrakios was sitting at the table reading a pile of documents. He rose and bowed. Theo didn't move from where he was standing by the window staring at the sea. Irini dropped onto a couch and addressed me.

"Stavrakios is summoning officials and Palace administrators to come before me and explain what is happening under their authority. I am making it clear that I am Regent and I speak for Constantine. I have discovered that several advisors were arranging to meet with Constantine without my presence. That will not happen again." She looked at Stavrakios. "Who is coming tomorrow?"

"Minister of the Imperial Post, Commander of the Palace Guard, and Master of the City Walls."

"What about the army commanders?" she demanded, sharply. "I want Mihalis the Dragon in here. And Tatzates. I want to hear the border situations. They reported to Leon after he was crowned. They will report to me."

"Of course, Empress. Who else?"

"The sons of the traitor Artavasdos. They joined their father against Emperor Constantine and started the Civil War. They are still living in the Hora Monastery where he confined them. I am certain that they were plotting with Dino's uncles. I want to know what they are up to."

Theo exploded. "Irini, you're not serious! They are old men—and impoverished! Emperor Constantine had them blinded. What possible harm could they do to you?"

"They are only in their sixties, no older than Patriarch Pavlos. And they can see perfectly well, I've been told; a few scars near the eyes. I want them here, face-to-face with me, telling me what they are plotting. Now, everyone leave, except Abbess Thekla."

We went into her bedchamber where her mute slave helped her into a long wool tunica of deep blue. She sat at her dressing table and began outlining her eyes with a tiny brush which she dipped into a small bottle of kohl.

"Consul Elpidios has returned from Sicily to offer me his condolences on Leon's death. You remember Elpidios; Leon accused him of having an affair with me. Fortunately, Leon's advisors persuaded him to send Elpidios to Sicily to be Consul, instead of executing him."

"Where are his wife and children?" I asked. "Weren't they imprisoned in some monastery?"

She draped a string of pearls around her neck, then exchanged them for a string of glittering green emeralds. "I told Stavrakios to have them released."

"Then his wife will be visiting with Captain Elpidios?" I pressed.

She glanced sharply at me. "You sound like Theo. Leon is dead and I am a widow. I can entertain whomever I please."

Her mute slave placed a carafe of red wine and two glasses on a low table in front of the fire. Nikitas the eunuch laid on another log and lit the candles. Irini began brushing her chestnut hair; it shone in the firelight. She looked so peaceful and happy—feelings she had never known, I realised. Why should she be denied what we all long for and need? I thought of my secret nights in Elias's arms in his room in Pendykion. I always felt stronger when I left there. And happy.

I spoke cautiously. "I hear you will be making new appointments. Is Constantine helping you decide? He is Emperor, even though he is too young to actually rule."

She smacked her hand on the table and glared at me. "I am Regent. I make the appointments." She went back to applying kohl around her eyes. "I have ordered everyone to collect their salaries in person so I can attach names to faces. Then I will announce my new appointments. They will be loyal to me and follow my orders. Constantine is supposed to call out the names but he can't say them properly so I am calling the appointees forward, myself."

"If you tell me the names, I can help Dino practice them."

"No," she said sharply. "Some nosy eunuch will overhear and everyone will know. I don't want any trouble beforehand."

"Is it wise to make changes so soon after your husband's death, Empress?" I persisted. I could understand Theo's alarm. She was making too many changes.

She scowled. "Stop sounding like Theo. He says I should wait until Constantine is older and let him make the new appointments. No. I will not wait. I am replacing every bastard who ever insulted me. Stavrakios and Aetios have suggested suitable replacements." She began smoothing her eyebrows with a tiny brush.

"I am sending Megalo home," I said, changing the subject.

She chuckled, good humour returned. "I knew that lazy girl wouldn't last long. I'll make Patriarch Pavlos approve her divorce when her father asks for it. Then he can try and get her dowry back from Fanis. I wish him luck with that. Did Brother Grigorios arrive?"

"He did, Empress. You're very generous." I hesitated. "Is this safe? Icons are still banned."

Her voice went hard. "I am Regent. Leon is dead but I am still Empress. I will send you an iconographer if I want." She looked at me in her mirror. "Aren't you going to ask me about why I arrested Constantine's two uncles?"

"Did they really conspire against you, Highness?"

"Of course they did. They have been conspiring against me in thought since the day I arrived from Athens. I am stopping them from turning their thoughts into action." She looked at me in her mirror. "That postal courier who comes out to Prinkypos, has he said anything about this? Are any army units coming to their rescue?"

"Elias has said nothing," I lied. "Shall I stay with Constantine in his chambers?"

She nodded. "Make the child stop weeping. He needs to grow up. In a few days, we will make the yearly inspection of the imperial granaries. Help him memorise the ceremony. Leave now, Elpidios will be here soon."

Constantine didn't need my help. He was reciting the ceremony to the eunuch who was Master of Ceremonies when I walked in and he sounded calm and confident. After the eunuch left, however, Constantine's confident manner slipped and he became an anxious nine-year-old.

"I'm worried I will do something wrong and upset Mama," he confided, sitting close beside me and holding my hand. "Listen to what we must do in the ceremony of the granaries: Mama and I enter the Great Hall. The patricians and other dignitaries and the imperial guards bow down to me. Mama and I get into the chariot. The city officials kiss my knees. The chariot driver kisses my feet. Two officials walk next to the chariot carrying the long gold rods that I must use to measure the grain. At the granaries, Mama gets out of the chariot first, then me. A notarios is standing by a table with the book that shows how much grain is stored. We walk through the granaries. I point to a bin and the surveyor pushes the gold rod into the grain and shows me how much is there. When we come out, I give the director of the granaries ten pounds of gold coins and a bolt of imperial silk. Same to the notarios."

"You know it perfectly, my sweet, like the Emperor that you are."

Tears of anger filled his eyes. "Auntie Thekla, my

advisors say that tomorrow I am supposed to announce the names of the new appointees. But Mama won't let me. She won't let me do anything. She interrupts me when I speak in the Consistory or when I am talking to foreign envoys." He put his hand over his eyes and began sobbing. I put my arms around him and he sobbed into my shoulder. "She is making me tonsure my uncles! And ordain them on the Day of Nativity! I can't do this, Auntie Thekla. I don't want to!"

I held him tight until his sobs faded. "Maybe she will change her mind," I managed.

He wiped his tears away with his hands and his young face hardened. With a pain in my heart, I saw that his innocent childhood face was gone. "Stavrakios and Aetios tell her lies about people in the Palace and the situation in the Empire—I have heard these lies. But Mama believes everything those two eunuchs tell her. My advisors are worried."

In the morning, Constantine's eunuchs came to dress him for the ceremony giving out salaries. I went to Chrysotriklinos Palace where I had received my stipends from Emperor Constantine and Emperor Leon. The Palace was close to the sea walls. Even though I had been there before, I still gasped at the gold and silver walls and pillars. I spotted Megalo's parents; Patrikios Leon was receiving his salary as a tax official. I came straight to the point.

"Megalo isn't suited to be a nun. You can come and get her."

Patrikia Constanta looked at me coldly. "What does Megalo want?"

"To be a nun," I admitted, reluctantly.

"Then keep her." She turned away.

I spoke equally coldly. "You wanted her to divorce and remarry. Empress Irini will make Patriarch Pavlos approve a divorce."

She whirled around. "I will not bring Megalo home and watch her mope around hoping that her scoundrel husband will come back. Tell her that if she comes home, she will divorce him and remarry. And you will give me back the money we paid for her room and board, down to the last copper follis."

I sighed with resignation, wondering what to do with Megalo. Maybe some convent in Constantinople would take her. Abbess Pulkeria certainly would not. Her nuns and novices worked even harder than mine.

Chrysotriklinos Palace was filled with people whispering or murmuring under their breath. Gone was the cheerful chatter of previous years when no one worried about their salaries. I spotted Theodore with his mother, Tisti. Brother Fanis was there, wearing monk's robes of rich blue silk. Consul Tarasios, who had taught Empress Irini how to navigate the channels of power when she first came to Constantinople, was talking to Brother Yiorgios and Brother Hilarion, the little monk who had tutored Irini when she was a princess. My stomach tightened when I saw Commander Mihalis the Dragon, the devil who had burnt down the Convent of Saint Emmelia while I was living there. I had barely survived. I remembered in my daily prayers the nuns who had perished.

I could see the lectern where Nikiforos, the accountant from the Finance Ministry, would call out the names in the ledger of the salary recipients. Beside the lectern was the long gold table where the purses of gold coins and bolts of silk would be placed for each salary recipient. Behind the table was the alcove where the imperial family sat during the ceremony. Theo came to stand beside me. "Only two thrones," he whispered.

I nodded. When Emperor Constantine and then Emperor Leon had sat in that alcove, there had been smaller thrones for Leon's five half-brothers and half-sister. Now two of the half-brothers were locked in a prison monastery and the half-sister was on her knees behind a convent Wall of Seclusion.

"Nikiforos, Accountant, Finance Ministry!" the Master of Ceremonies shouted.

The thin man came in followed by two scribes who placed the big ledger on the lectern.

"Constantine, Emperor, Empress Irini, Empress and Regent!" The guards swung open the big doors.

Constantine had sat through this ceremony since he was a child but he looked frightened and overwhelmed. His lips were white. Empress Irini waited with a patient smile while he climbed up on the big throne, then she seated herself. Whispers floated around me, "Look at those jewels!" "Is that tunica solid gold?" Irini's eyes roved the crowd, picking out faces. Her eyes rested on me. I stiffened. Was that fear I felt? Were others feeling the same?

Accountant Nikiforos began calling out the names, but there was no easy chatter as when Emperor Constantine had supervised the yearly salaries. There weren't even the stiff smiles of the four years of Emperor Leon's salary ceremonies. Empress Irini said nothing when the army and navy commanders came forward and dropped to one knee. To others, she gave a brief nod but these were few. I was last, the least important. I backed away holding my small purse and stood beside Theo. His handsome face was tense with worry.

"Here we go," he muttered.

Empress Irini rose and held out her hand to the Master of Ceremonies. With a low bow, he presented a small parchment. She spoke without looking at it in her hand. Her voice rang out over the silent room. "Now hear my new appointments for imperial posts!"

Theo whispered under his breath. "She's calling the names herself. Mistake. She should not flaunt Palace protocol. The Emperor or the Master of Ceremonies is supposed to call the names."

"Minister of the Post and Transportation, I name Stavrakios, currently Head of my household."

She gave a tiny smile at the wave of shocked murmurs. Theo muttered under his breath. "A position of real power. He will have a say in foreign affairs. Given to a eunuch with no experience."

"Minister of the Military Budget, I name Ioannis from my household staff."

Again came Theo's hiss. "Another eunuch elevated above his experience. This lowly eunuch will control the entire military budget of the Asiatic themes. All the commanders appointed by Emperor Constantine and Emperor Leon will have their budgets dictated by him."

I looked at Commander Mihalis the Dragon and Commander Tatzates. They looked grim.

"To the rank of patrikios and all its privileges, I name army officers Theodoros and Theophilos," Irini continued.

Theo muttered in my ear, "Seasoned officers, but Theodoros is a eunuch. Another eunuch elevated to patrikios."

"Brother Yiorgios of Jerusalem I name as my Ecclesiastical Advisor."

Theo whispered. "A monk with no duties except to be at her beck and call. That means Brother Yiorgios is her spy. Be careful what you say when he is near."

There were other appointments that Theo said nothing about, just tightened his lips.

That evening after Constantine was asleep, I went to Empress Irini's chambers to tell her I was leaving in the morning. She was smug and delighted with herself.

"I am doing things my own way, Thekla. No one can tell me what to do."

"Men will always tell women what to do," I muttered. I didn't ask her to send me to Prinkypos in the imperial yacht and she didn't offer.

I told Dino goodbye in the morning with a lump in my throat.

"Don't go, Auntie Thekla," he begged, weeping.

"You will come out to Prinkypos in the spring. I have to make sure that we have enough food to last us through the winter."

"I will make sure you always have enough to eat, Auntie Thekla," he said solemnly.

Theo walked me out Chalke Gate. Swarms of Palace employees were hurrying to their office buildings and workshops inside the walls of the Great Palace. Theo looked downcast and worried. "Irini has never been cautious or prudent, and she is making grave mistakes. It is customary for emperors to appoint eunuchs to Palace administrative positions. Eunuchs can have no children so they cannot pass on their positions and develop family fiefdoms. But Irini has appointed eunuchs with no experience to powerful roles. She will lose the loyalty of the people who should have kept those posts."

"Dino says that she interrupts him during meetings with his advisors in the Consistory."

He gave a frustrated sigh. "I tell her that Constantine needs to have a voice in the Consistory. He is nearly ten and he has been in those meetings since he sat on his grandfather's knee. He is being educated to be Emperor and he is starting his military training. He is already good with a short sword. Yes, Irini needs to show her advisors that she has the knowledge and experience to be Regent, but Constantine is old enough to take on some responsibilities. Then he will be a capable ruler when he is eighteen."

"Given her nature, and how she distrusts everyone at the Palace, I don't see her letting Constantine do anything." I glanced around to make sure no one could overhear. "Dino says that Stavrakios and Aetios lie to Irini and she believes them."

"She trusts those two brutes absolutely!" Theo burst out. "They are feared in the Palace. Everyone knows they will do anything to get power and wealth. Stavrakios strolls around in a disdainful way as if he were on the throne and not a castrated excuse for a human being."

I climbed on the ferry to Chalkidon and sat on deck letting the fierce wind clear my troubled thoughts. In Chalkidon, I bought cheese and bread and joined some nuns walking to Pendykion. The wind pushed us along the sea road and, despite the short autumn day, we entered the passage under the Pendykion walls before dusk. I spotted Elias unloading bundles of mail from a mail coach.

"Cousin! I've been expecting you!" he called for the benefit of the postal couriers and passers-by.

I was asleep in his bed when the aroma of stew rich with carrots and leeks woke me. We ate by the wavery light of a tallow candle.

"Let's take another journey together," he said. "Let's walk over the mountains of Bithynia to the double monastery of Saint Emmelia, as we did years ago. The monks and nuns are restoring it—those who survived the blaze," he added.

I smiled at him. "A lovely thought, but you and I cannot leave our responsibilities. Besides, those nuns knew that I never took the vows. I cannot take the risk that they will discover that I am the Abbess of an imperial convent."

"Then we will sleep under a blanket of stars," he smiled.

That night, curled up against him, I dreamed that I was inside the church at Saint Emmelia convent, gazing at the icons on the pillars and the wall icons of saints helping the villagers plant, harvest, and carry the icon of Saint Emmelia in the village procession. My dream moved inside the little church in my own convent courtyard. I saw a life-size icon of my name saint, Saint Thekla First Woman Martyr and Equal to the Apostles, on the pillar by the door. I saw the wall icons of villagers and women saints working together. I awoke and stared up into the dark rafters, listening to Elias breathing softly. Saint Thekla was sending me a message. Now I knew what to tell Brother Grigorios to paint on the walls and pillars of our little convent church.

Saint Thekla had guided my steps ever since our village priest baptised me and placed her tiny icon on my infant body. Following the priest's brave defiance of the ban on icons, I had carried her my whole adult life, tied into the corner of my scarf. She had guided me safely to Constantinople to search for my betrothed. She had found me work and a place to live. She had brought me out of prison to Prinkypos Island and she had caused Irini to appoint me as Abbess of the Convent of the Theotokos. I would tell Brother Grigorios to paint the image of Saint Thekla on the pillar just inside the door and to cover the walls with scenes of village women and saints together herding sheep, tending the sick, cleaning floors—all the tasks that women do together. The next morning, I climbed off Elias's boat on Prinkypos and gave Brother Grigorios his instructions.

The week after Nativity, a cold sun glinted off the snow. Sister Filothei, Aspasia and I were visiting Father Dimitrios and his wife to bring them the Nativity bread that Aspasia had baked. Elias sailed in and settled next to Brother Grigorios by the fire.

"Empress Irini did what she said," Elias reported, frowning into the coals. "On the Day of the Nativity, I watched Constantine stand before hundreds of people in the Church of Holy Wisdom of God and chant the ritual to ordain his uncles as clergy—guided by Patriarch Pavlos."

"Empress Irini was there, herself?" Father Dimitrios cut in, disbelieving.

"She sat in the imperial box in jet black mourning clothes with a black headscarf covering her forehead down to her eyebrows and wrapped around her throat and chin. She looked like a nun." He looked at me, with my scarf around my neck, my hair free. "Some nuns."

I felt ill. "I thought she would be lenient."

"Has our Empress ever been lenient?" His voice grew hot with anger. "She opened the church so everyone could watch the humiliation of those two young men. Christoforos and Nikiforos were dragged in wearing monk's robes and sandals. Their heads were shaved in the shape of a cross. They were forced to their knees in front of poor Constantine. He looked smothered under those heavy ceremonial robes. Patriarch Pavlos coached him word-by-word through the ordination. Both he and the Patriarch looked like they would collapse. Then Patriarch Pavlos had to talk Nikiforos and Christoforos through saying the Eucharist. Technically, they are now priests and can never be emperor."

"She did it to protect Dino," I blurted. "Emperor Constantine had warned her that his sons by Empress Evdokia would try to take the throne after he died. He made Irini promise to protect Dino and make sure he sat on the throne."

They stared at me in stunned silence.

"I heard him say it, myself," I repeated, hesitant to defend Irini for her cruelty to those two young men, but unable to remain silent. "Irini became ill after Dino was born. The Emperor came to her bedchamber. He told her she had to recover so she could make sure that Dino became Emperor."

Father Dimitrios shook his head. "Even so, how pitiless to make a nine-year-old forcibly ordain his own uncles."

"She had no choice," I said stubbornly. "If she had exiled them, they would have gathered an army and come to take the throne from Constantine."

Elias cut in. "Not from Constantine. If the brothers were conspiring against Irini—which I doubt—they would have taken her off the throne and put Constantine in his rightful place."

"They would have taken the throne," I argued. "Their own father predicted it!"

"Thekla, think!" Elias snapped, exasperated. "When Leon became Emperor, he crowned Constantine as his Co-emperor. Remember that gathering of 'the people'—army officers and patricians who had received money as a gift from Leon when he was crowned? Stavrakios and Aetios had gathered them in the Augustaion and led them in a vow to be loyal to Leon and his descendants. If Nikiforos and Christoforos had tried to put themselves on the throne, those very people would have marched into the Palace, arrested them, and put Constantine on the throne—and named some army commander as regent—probably Mihalis the Dragon. If Nikiforos and Christoforos had really conspired to take the throne—

which I don't believe—they were taking it from Irini, not from Constantine."

"Then why didn't the army drag Irini from the throne when she arrested Dino's two uncles?" I was still trying to justify the actions of the woman to whom I had sworn loyalty.

"Because the army doesn't care a whit about Nikiforos and Christoforos. They are not in the line of succession. The army only cares that young Constantine is safe until he turns eighteen and takes the throne. As long as Empress Irini doesn't harm Constantine, the army will stay out of the throne room."

He was right. It took my breath away, how right he was. But I made one last protest. "You don't think that the army will rise against her and crown one of their officers?" This was what Theo had feared.

He shook his head. "Taking the throne would start a civil war. Easier would be to simply replace Irini with a new regent."

"Those poor young men, forced to be priests against their will," sighed Sister Filothei.

Father Dimitrios shook his head. "A forced ordination is no ordination. They are not priests in God's eyes."

Elias nodded. "Now they will truly conspire against Irini. And the other supposed conspirators will conspire against her in exile. They will return to join Dino's uncles against Irini. She has created a lot of trouble for herself."

"At least she didn't have the brothers executed for treason," said Father Dimitrios.

"She knows better," retorted Elias. "Even though they are not in line for the throne, they are popular army officers. There would have been riots in the streets."

"How are the people of Constantinople taking this?" Father Dimitrios asked.

Elias stared moodily into the fire. "People are angry. Crowds gather in front of Chalke Gate and shout 'injustice'. The city is dark. The colonnades and stoa are draped in mourning for Emperor Leon. There aren't any Nativity banners on Mesi Street. Empress Irini sent out the usual Nativity hams and cheese wheels to the Forum of Constantine and the Forum of the Ox, and she and Constantine made many visits to poorhouses and orphanages and hospitals. Other than that, she has stayed inside the Great Palace."

"Whatever is she plotting next, I wonder?" murmured Father Dimitrios, surprising me. He had always spoken with awe of Irini's beauty, wit, and strength.

"Whatever it is, it will be unexpected," replied Elias darkly.

Chapter IV

For the next two years, Constantine came out to Prinkypos only for the occasional hard-earned rest from his rigorous training to be Emperor of the Roman Empire of the East. He would leap off the imperial yacht shouting for his friends, and run off with them to kick the ball around the plateia or swim in the sea. Empress Irini always came with him and spent her days pacing the island's goat paths or reading in the big chair under our grape vine that the village carpenter had built for her.

The June after Dino had turned eleven, Empress Irini stomped off the yacht after him, in foul humour. She nodded curtly to Brother Grigorios and the children who had run forward with flowers, and marched into Saint Nikolaos church with Father Dimitrios to give a quick thanks for her safe arrival. I waited outside with her mute slave and four guards. Dino was off with his friends, his fair head among their dark ones. My heart swelled proudly to see his muscles from his sword training and other military exercises. As I followed Irini up the lane to the convent, I felt sad to lose my little boy.

Irini flung herself onto the bench against the convent wall by the cemetery at the top of the lane and glared at the harbour below and the green islands that spilled out at our feet like someone had flung a handful of green figs. While her mute slave took her bundles into the convent and her guards lounged further down the lane, I stood, waiting for the outburst.

"Elpidios is a traitor!" she burst out, twisting her scarf around her fingers. "He lied to me, Thekla! I re-appointed him Consul of Sicily and he left last month. Now Stavrakios tells me that Elpidios had conspired with Dino's uncles to seize the throne! Stavrakios says I should have tonsured and exiled Elpidios along with them. Or had all three of them executed for treason!"

"Can you be sure that Stavrakios has the real story?" I asked, cautiously.

She glared at me. "Are you accusing him of lying?"

Of course I was. Stavrakios was a cunning manipulator and he was getting rid of Elpidios who had the love of Irini. I felt no pity for Consul Elpidios. He was an opportunist and a snob. He had returned from his Consul post in Sicily to attend Leon's funeral and had blithely picked up his relationship with Irini where he had left off—no matter that he had a wife and children. Still, he had put a smile on Irini's face and for this I was grudgingly grateful. During the four tense years between the deaths of Emperor Constantine and Emperor Leon, she had little reason to laugh. So I took up his defence.

"Why would Consul Elpidios conspire against you?

He had your confidence and your friendship. After Emperor Leon died, you kindly released his wife and children from the monastery prison."

She wiped her tears with her fingers. "Stavrakios said Elpidios needed money to bring his wife and children to Sicily. For this, he joined the conspiracy."

"Did Nikiforos or Christoforos name him specifically?"

"No. I had them interrogated. They lied, of course. Every word from their lips is a lie. From the moment I walked off that warship to marry Leon, his half-brothers have tried to get rid of me. I should have had them blinded when the conspiracy was fresh in everyone's mind."

Her hatred of Constantine's uncles worried me. Hatred is bred by fear but she had nothing to fear from those young men. The two eldest were in a prison monastery and the three others were too young to cause trouble. "Can someone else tell you more about this situation?"

"I have sent an army officer to bring Elpidios back. I cannot allow a traitor to be Consul of Sicily and Calabria—especially with Pope Adrianos eyeing them for his own."

"Did Stavrakios recommend this officer?" I asked, suspicious.

"He did, in fact. I had elevated Theodoros to patrikios at the ceremony when I named Stavrakios as Minister of the Post."

I remembered the ceremony. Theo had muttered that the officer was a eunuch with some military experience. "What if Consul Elpidios refuses to come back?"

"Oh, he will come. I have locked his wife and children back in the monastery. Elpidios will have to beg me personally for their release. I will have the truth in two or three months, when Elpidios stands in front of me and explains why he conspired against me."

There are moments when the veil of time parts and we can see into the future. At that moment, I saw Irini step onto the wrong path. She was not a good judge of men. Or women. How could she be? She had lost her parents at an early age, grown up in the unwelcome household of her army commander uncle, and reached the age of seventeen without an offer of marriage. Her uncle had handed her over to Emperor Constantine who took her to Constantinople and married her to his son who didn't want her. Elpidios had been the one bright spot in her life. Poor Elpidios. His crime was his handsome face and charming manners. Of course Stavrakios was lying about the conspiracy. I tried another tactic.

"Does Dino think that Elpidios was part of the conspiracy?" I asked, knowing that Dino loathed Stavrakios.

Empress Irini erupted in fury. "Constantine will say anything against Stavrakios—and me. He wanted to come here alone today—without me. He doesn't understand that he and I must always be seen together, to show that we share the throne. He wants to stay here during Easter. This is impossible. The Emperor leads the Easter procession and ceremonies. During Holy Week, we visit hospitals, orphanages, schools—together. After Easter, there is the procession to Evdomon Palace to review the army in the parade ground. This too, he wants to do alone. He cannot. I am Regent. We go together."

We could hear the faint shouts of Constantine and

his friends. "He still plays children's games! The son of Caliph al-Mahdi was commanding an army at his age. He is only five years older and our spies in the Caliphate are calling him a military genius."

"Constantine says you don't allow him full military training."

"He's too young and small for his age. He will be injured."

"He says you don't allow him to speak in the Consistory with the senators and patricians. He could give his opinion; he has good tutors."

"Good tutors don't always make good emperors. Look at his father. No, what my son needs is knowledge of the Empire. I will take him to Thessaloniki and the western themes. There is a beautiful church of Saint Dimitrios in Thessaloniki. I saw it when we stopped there, when Emperor Constantine brought me to Constantinople. I want to commission a mosaic for it."

My back was aching from standing and I stealthily eased down onto a slab of stone over a grave shaft. She didn't notice but went on talking.

"There is something else that Constantine will complain to you about. I have sent ambassadors to King Charles of the Franks to propose a marriage between his daughter Rotrud and Constantine."

I gasped and my heart twisted, thinking of my little boy as a husband and father. "He is only eleven!"

She shrugged. "Rotrud is younger. They will wed when she is thirteen. Imagine, Thekla, my son will be Emperor of the Romans of the East and also King of the Franks! He and I will control the world! I have sent the betrothal proposal to Rome. Charles is there for Easter, his ambassadors tell me. Pope Adrianos will hear of it. The old goat will be terrified."

"Why do you care about the Pope, Empress?"

"Because a union between me and Charles of the Franks will stop Pope Adrianos from going after our lands in Calabria and Sicily. The popes have been coveting those lands since before my father-in-law was on the throne. When Leon became Emperor, Pope Adrianos had the temerity to issue Roman coins with his own wrinkled face on them instead of Leon and his father. I told Leon to send him an order to put our emperors' images back on their coins. Leon refused, the coward."

I had been with Dino in the nursery and had heard the angry shouting. Emperor Leon had thrown a glass vase against the wall. Irini continued, her voice filled with anger.

"Now Pope Adrianos has enacted some sort of papal edict that people must remember King Charles of the Franks along with the Emperor of the Romans of the East in their daily prayers. I have to accept this in silence because we need Charles as our ally. Emperor Constantine always had good relations with him, even when Charles attacked Lombardia and Constantine granted sanctuary to the son of the Lombard king. At that time, Constantine bestowed on King Charles the title of patrikios. Constantine told me that he was telling Charles that they were still allies. As a Christian, Constantine was bound to give sanctuary to another Christian."

"Did King Charles understand this?" I asked, curious about the dealings between rulers.

She shrugged. "I reminded him in my letter proposing the betrothal. Another issue has come up where Charles and I must stand together against the Pope. Listen to this nonsense: Pope Adrianos wants to change our system of dating the years. Year one is the year of Creation. Everyone accepts this. But that heretic Pope Adrianos wants year one to be the birth of Christ. Absurd! Everyone knows the birth of Christ was the year five thousand five hundred and nine."

I was confused. "Why does it matter when Our Lord was born? The importance is that He was born, not when."

"Religion has nothing to do with it," Irini snapped impatiently. "This is another ploy by the Pope to dominate the world. If he can make everyone use his system of measuring time, then imagine what other strange beliefs he will force down our throats! Well, I for one will not bend my knee to his time system!"

Constantine was coming up the lane, dusty and smiling. We entered the convent gates and gazed at the basilica that Empress Irini was having built in the pasture just outside the walls around the convent buildings. When the convent was being restored, Irini had wanted to tear down our tiny church in the convent courtyard and build the basilica there. I had persuaded her that a larger basilica could be built in the pasture and that people from the village and other islands could come there without disturbing the peace of the convent. Construction had begun right after Emperor Leon's death. Now, the outline of the rising walls showed the large size. It would have two aisles and a loft. The crypt was dug and lined with stone. Irini smiled in satisfaction.

"Leon refused every time I told him that the island deserved more than the Church of Saint Nikolaos by the harbour and the little convent church. How annoyed he would be to see it now."

Constantine ran into the kitchen to throw his arms around Aspasia, as always, and Empress Irini and I strolled through the orchard and vegetable gardens. She settled in the big wooden chair under the grape vine and watched the baby chicks scurry around like bits of yellow fluff. Aspasia brought a plate of warm flatbread and a bowl of chickpea paste sprinkled with pine nuts and our red sumac powder that we ground from the berries we picked from the bushes against the convent wall. Empress Irini tore off a piece of flatbread and scooped up some paste.

"Theodore tells me that Fanis has been tonsured," she commented with her mouth full. "At the Polychronos Monastery. Do you know the place?"

"I've heard it is a rich monastery across the Propontis Sea, near the monastery where Theodore's uncle is Abbot."

"Theodore says that Fanis wants to build his own monastery, to be called the Monastery of the Metamorphosis. I assume he will pay for it with Megalo's dowry. He doesn't have to give it back to Megalo's father unless they are divorced. Which he won't allow, I'm sure. Theodore never ceases his praise of Fanis. 'A man of great reason with a mind of scholarship and full of divine knowledge', he calls him."

"Theodore loves big words with little meaning."

She laughed. "Theodore will become a monk, I'm afraid. I must find a way to keep him in Constantinople. His witty chatter entertains me and he will keep me informed about what the monks around the Empire are plotting."

She stared over the low part of the wall at the glittering sea. "I worry about what Caliph al-Mahdi is up to. Our spies report that his son Harun has not been seen in months—off somewhere training his army, they think. I sent a messenger to Commander Mihalis the Dragon and Commander Tatzates to report to me on the readiness of our troops. Neither has replied. Do they not understand that I am Regent! I am their commander!"

They understand only too well, I thought.

Later that summer, Caliph al-Mahdi sent his commander, Abd al-Kebir, over our border where he went up against The Dragon and Tatzates—and Irini's new appointee, Ioannis the eunuch. Elias scoffed when he brought us the news.

"Empress Irini has made a household eunuch first into a fiscal official and now overall commander of the combined imperial armies. He has no experience in either. We may soon hear that he has died with our own arrows in his back."

Our armies fought Abd al-Kebir all through the heat of August and into September. Irini and Constantine stayed in Constantinople. Finally, Elias brought the welcome news that our forces had defeated al-Kebir at the battle of Melon. The next day, Megalo shouted that the imperial yacht was coming. I ran to look. Irini was on deck with Constantine who was waving madly. I ran for the harbour with Sister Matrona and Sister Evanthia to welcome them. As we watched the Empress stride down the gangplank, Sister Matrona shook her head.

"Who will she battle next?" Sister Matrona muttered. "Caliph al-Mahdi or Mihalis the Dragon?"

Chapter V

Harun al-Rashid was whom Irini fought next—the sixteen-year-old military genius son of Caliph al-Mahdi. The next spring, we awoke to the faint clicks of horses' hooves on cobblestones floating across the narrow strip of water between us and the mainland. Staring desperately over our wall, we could make out tiny horses and soldiers moving along the coastal road away from Constantinople. Fishing boats loaded with people were sailing towards us and the other islands. We all ran down to the harbour. Elias was climbing out of the mail boat with three grim men wearing the tunicas of postal couriers. Elias jerked his head bleakly at the lines of soldiers.

"Harun al-Rashid has invaded with his combined armies. That's one of his armies over there, marching to attack Nikomidia. Mihalis the Dragon is waiting there with an army of thirty thousand. Harun himself is attacking the city of Chrysopolis—right across the most narrow part of the Propontis Sea from Constantinople. If Chrysopolis falls, Harun will load his men on the barges docked there and sail across the Propontis to attack the walls of Constantinople."

How can I describe our weeks of terror? A mere strip of water lay between us and foreign soldiers who would drag us from our convent. Elias and the fishermen slid back and forth at night bringing people fleeing the coastal towns. We took the women and children into the convent and found beds in the dormitory, the library, and the classrooms. Aspasia and Sister Matrona and I met daily to find ways to feed them from our dwindling supplies. Elias came up to report.

"Empress Irini has sent Stavrakios to Nikomidia with Antonios, Commander of the Palace Guard, and rein-forcements. Our army matches Harun's—thirty-thou-sand strong on both sides."

"All we can do is pray for a victory to our soldiers," Father Dimitrios muttered.

Chrysopolis held fast but our prayers for The Dragon and his armies went unanswered. Elias wept as he gave us the news.

"The Great Harun himself went to Nikomidia to lead the battle. Fifteen thousand of our soldiers lie dead."

We were terrified, not knowing where Harun would move his armies next. The villagers brought their sheep and belongings up to the convent, as if our walls could stop an invading army. I checked and rechecked our supplies. I was on the verge of showing Father Dimitrios how to get down to the secret room below my study when Elias returned, exhausted but exultant.

"The invasion is over," he announced, beaming at our desperate faces in the plateia. "Commander Tatzates, clever man, laid an ambush and captured the great Harun. But that's not the best part of the story."

The details were so astounding that Elias had to repeat them over and over. "Commander Tatzates hates Stavrakios and he saw a way to get rid of him. Tatzates made a secret pact with the captured Harun. Tatzates promised Harun his freedom—and Stavrakios as his prisoner—if Harun would grant Tatzates safe-conduct to the Caliphate with his wife and children. Harun agreed."

"Commander Tatzates defected to the Caliph?" Disbelief showed on everyone's faces.

Elias nodded. "Tatzates hates Empress Irini as much as he hates Stavrakios. He sent a message to Stavrakios that Harun was ready to negotiate a peace. Stavrakios and two army officers came to the camp where Tatzates was holding Harun prisoner. It was a trap. Tatzates and Harun's men took them prisoner and are now holding them for ransom."

Father Dimitrios broke the stunned silence. "What if Empress Irini doesn't pay ransom?"

"She will pay. Stavrakios is keeping her on the throne."

Irini paid. We got the details in July when she came out to the island with Constantine. He was twelve then, a handsome, fair-haired young man with a quiet voice and the muscles and posture of a soldier—shoulders back, feet firmly planted. But that day his normally sweet smile was a grim line. Empress Irini was thirty that year and more beautiful than ever, but her face was drawn and pale. The three of us sat in my study with the shutters closed against the July heat.

"I had to ransom Stavrakios and those two idiots captured with him," she said in a low, hard voice. "Fools! Then I had to sue for peace. The terms are humiliating. One hundred and sixty thousand gold nomismata. Per year! And hundreds of bolts of imperial silk. Caliph al-Mahdi promises not to invade as long as we keep paying."

"So much gold to save that swine!" Constantine swore.

Irini glared at him, then her eyes filled with tears. "Thekla, you can't imagine the terror of having Harun directly across the Propontis! Thank God that Chrysopolis held fast. If Harun had captured any barges, he would have climbed through the broken wall below the Great Palace!"

"Here on the island, we had no army to protect us," I said with an edge in my voice.

"You are not Empress!" she shouted in fury. Constantine cut her off in an icy voice.

"Nikiforos from the Finance Ministry stood up before a meeting in the Consistory and said my mother had made a grave mistake to ransom Stavrakios. He said death would have given that incompetent pig some measure of honour. He wants my mother to confiscate Stavrakios's property and send him into exile. I agreed, and I stood up and said so."

My heart filled with joy to hear him speak with such authority. I hid my smile from Irini as he went on with scathing anger.

"My mother won't listen. She has refused to punish that moron in any way."

"Because Tatzates tricked him and turned traitor!"

Empress Irini shouted. "Our spies say that the Caliph has already given Tatzates some high military post."

Constantine's shout equalled hers. "Tatzates should be rewarded for trying to rid the empire of a lying, devious, money-grubbing eunuch. I'm surprised more commanders haven't defected after you raised him to high office. One day I will face Tatzates across a battle-field—and my death will be on your head!"

His words stilled her. Constantine turned to me. He lowered his voice but the anger was still there. "Auntie Thekla, my mother's greatest skill is her ability to ignore good advice. Listen to this: a group of army officers, showing great courage, requested an audience with my mother and me. They said that Stavrakios is unworthy of being Minister of the Post and Transportation. They said that no one in the army or the Ministry of Foreign Affairs trusts him. They want him exiled back to Kappa-dokia where he came from. They say that he is a greedy, power-hungry liar who would grab the throne from my mother and me except that he cannot because he is a eunuch. My mother has ignored these officers. She will not even revoke his title of patrikios."

"Consul Tarasios trusts Stavrakios as much as I do," Irini snarled.

"Tarasios would eat camel dung if you told him," he snapped back.

The Empress spoke through her teeth. "I am giving Stavrakios a chance to redeem himself. This autumn, I am sending him on campaign against the Slavs."

Constantine gaped at her in disbelief. "Mother, the Treasury cannot afford a campaign to anywhere. We have lost too many men and weapons to Harun. And we're paying his yearly tribute."

"Which I am considering stopping." She poured herself a glass of elderberry wine and drank it down.

Constantine turned to me. "She makes mistake after mistake. Listen to another. My mother has betrothed me to the daughter of King Charles of the Franks. Rotrud is her name. The negotiations have been going on for some time without my knowledge. King Charles has agreed. We have just received his signed documents."

I stared at him in dismay. "Will you go to live with the Franks?"

"I don't know," he said with a savage look at his mother. "I don't even know what this creature looks like."

"Our ambassadors in Aachen say she is beautiful and sweet-tempered," said Irini.

"All princesses are beautiful and sweet-tempered," snarled Constantine.

"They also write that Charles has educated her with all his children. She is talented in embroidery, spinning and weaving."

"If they said nothing of her literacy, this means she cannot read."

"You are not marrying her for her wit," Irini said, "although I assume she has some intelligence, given her father. I am sending three eunuchs to teach her our language and customs. They will send me regular reports about her—and what goes on in the court of Charles."

"The marriage may never happen, anyway," Constantine said, with a dark look at Irini. "Pope Adrianos is against it. Our ambassadors in Charles's court in Aachen got their hands on a letter the Pope was sending to Charles. A woman cannot legally sign a betrothal document, the Pope wrote."

Empress Irini made a face. "The old goat is just writing that to make me bend my knee to him and beg for his approval for this marriage. Well, I won't beg. I will get around him. He is obsessed with forcing the Orthodox Church to match the beliefs of the Latin church. He wants us to bring icons back into worship. Obsessed men are easily manipulated because you know what they want. I have a plan." She smiled and poured herself more elderberry wine.

Constantine narrowed his eyes. "Is this about the ecumenical council that my eunuchs tell me you are discussing with Tarasios?"

She nodded. "I will tell the Pope—and Charles—that I plan to convene an ecumenical council of bishops. I will tell him that I will hand-pick the bishops who will vote to merge the beliefs of Constantinople with Rome and bring back icons. That will make the old goat approve your marriage to Rotrud."

"You don't have the power," said Constantine flatly. "A regent cannot convene a council of bishops. Only an emperor can do this. I have asked my advisors and they are certain on this point. And I won't do it. It will cause nothing but trouble."

That was the day when I saw the path that Irini of Athens was taking to power, the day my loyalties began to slip over to Constantine in the way that the silver light of the evening sky slips over the sea.

Empress Irini leaned forward, her voice low and intent. "Listen to me, my sweet Dino. If you and I convene this council, many good things will happen. The Pope will stop objecting to your marriage. Charles will stop the Pope from invading our lands in Sicily and Calabria. The monks will love us because they have never stopped painting icons and now they can paint them freely. The people will love us because their icons will be back in their cottages. It's already happening, anyway. Reports are coming from around the Empire that icons are appearing in village churches. Why not make this official? Dino, my heart, let us convene an ecumenical council and formally reinstate icons. Emperor Constantine locked three hundred and eleven bishops in Hieria Palace for six months until they voted to ban icons. We will do the same, in reverse."

"You are bringing back icons only to keep good relations with foreigners," Constantine accused her. "You don't care what our own people want."

She threw up her hands. "My dear boy, what does it matter, the reason? What is an icon anyway but a bit of painted wood?"

I interrupted. "Father Dimitrios says that an icon is a link to the infinite divine, a window into heaven."

Irini turned to me. "Thekla, when the people in the village below go into the church by the harbour and gaze into the face of Saint Nikolaos on the icon that Father Dimitrios has brought out from hiding, do they see a link to an infinite divine? They do not. They see Saint Nikolaos. They ask him to cure their sick mother or find their lost goat. You yourself speak to your icon as your friend. I have heard you. An icon is whatever a person needs it to be."

She leaned back in her chair with a self-satisfied smile. "I will invite Pope Adrianos to send delegates from Rome to my ecumenical council. The old fool will think he has broken the will of a woman and forced me to bring the Eastern Church in line with the Latin church. He will put his papal seal on Constantine's marriage to the daughter of Charles of the Franks. And Charles will send his armies to help us defeat Caliph al-Mahdi and his son Harun al-Rashid."

Constantine and I looked at each other. It was obvious that she had already written to the Pope and King Charles of the Franks. There was nothing Constantine could do.

A few days later, Stavrakios arrived on the mail boat with Elias and handed Irini a letter. She sat in the plateia with him for some time. I didn't go down, even though it would have meant chatting with Elias. I loathed Stavrakios and even being near him made me itch to pull out my knife. I watched them from the top of the lane until Stavrakios got back in the boat and Irini stormed up the lane. She flung herself on the bench beside the cemetery and burst into tears.

"Elpidios refuses to come home. He told the army officer I sent that he had nothing to do with any conspiracy. The Sicilians won't hand him over—even though Sicily is part of the Empire! Oh, Thekla, if Elpidios were innocent, he would explain to me, personally. I loved him, Thekla," she sobbed into her handkerchief. "I opened my heart to him. He held me in his arms. And all the time, he was plotting to destroy me. Is there a man anywhere who can be trusted?" She fumbled a papyrus letter from her pocket and thrust it at me.

I read it through twice with a frown. "This is written by Stavrakios. He is telling you what the army officer told him about what Elpidios said."

"Yes, I know," she said irritably.

"Is there no letter from Elpidios? He wrote to you when he was Consul. Why not now?"

She snatched the letter from my hands. "Are you accusing Stavrakios of lying?"

Of course I was. I didn't blame Elpidios for refusing to come home. Stavrakios would make sure that he ended up in prison. "Perhaps the army officer didn't report Elpidios's words accurately to Stavrakios. Can you write to Elpidios and demand his explanation in writing? Commander Elpidios is highly respected, Empress. Never has he been accused of anything but loyalty to you."

"I will not beg him to write!" she shouted, drawing the attention of her guards lounging in the shade down the lane. She lowered her voice. "Elpidios very likely has acquired a Sicilian wife and children. That's why the Sicilians won't give him up. They will change their tune when they see the fleet I am sending to bring him back."

I gaped at her. "A naval fleet? To bring back one man?"

"Stavrakios assures me that they will simply sail in, collect Elpidios, and sail back. Stavrakios has advised me to promise the commander the post of Consul of Sicily if he brings Elpidios back."

"Stavrakios recommended this man, I assume."

"Do not question me!" she shouted. "Stavrakios brought the order and I have just signed it. The Treasury can afford a small naval campaign. I am Empress. I can spend the funds as I choose."

Constantine was now too old to stay in the convent, so the Palace Master Builder had built cottages for him and his guards in the village. He spent his days with his friends, fishing, mending nets, or kicking a ball around the plateia. The next morning I went down and told him that Irini had sent a fleet to bring Elpidios back to Constantinople. He threw up his arms with an anguished groan.

"Sending warships to attack our own people! To capture a married man who has done her no harm except to be the victim of Stavrakios's lies. She won't listen to me or any of her advisors. The Master of City Walls says we must repair our sea walls. They were broken during my grandfather's time when an iceberg floated down the Bosporus and smashed into them. When Harun attacked the last time, my mother was terrified that he would come straight through the gap in our walls. Now she claims that we lack money for repairs. Of course we have no money. She ransomed Stavrakios and we are paying tribute to Caliph al-Mahdi to keep the peace. One day al-Mahdi will want more than gold. He will want us under his rule."

Empress Irini went back to Constantinople after a few weeks, but Constantine stayed for the summer. Every day we walked by the sea. We scraped barnacles off rocks and ate them raw off the tips of our knives as we had done when he was a child.

"The Palace is suffocating me," Constantine complained, echoing his mother's complaint from years before. "The only thing I like is my military training. But what's the point of learning to fight when my mother won't let me go on campaign?"

Elias joined our walks when he brought dispatches for Constantine from his advisors and gossipy letters from his Palace eunuchs. We settled on the beach and Constantine read them, shaking his head.

"My mother has persuaded the Consistory and the Finance Ministry to pay for the Slav campaign that she wants Stavrakios to lead. She is telling everyone that she wants to recapture our lands that my great-grandfather lost to the Slavs. What she really wants is to redeem Stavrakios's reputation after he walked into that trap set by Harun and Commander Tatzates. That won't happen. Stavrakios has never headed a military unit, much less a campaign. This will be a disaster."

Elias shrugged. "The real commanders will lead the campaign."

"And get no credit from my mother, which they will resent and remember." Constantine went on reading. "She has promised Stavrakios a Triumph in the Hippodrome if he pushes back the Slavs." He looked at us with cold anger in his young eyes. "I will pray that Stavrakios dies in the first battle—and I will not be the only one with such prayers."

Chapter VI

Stavrakios, that lucky swine, was victorious. That autumn, he took back all the territory that Emperor Leon the Isaurian had lost to the Slavs so long ago that only the imperial mapmakers knew where the border had been. It was all forest, anyway. I saw it later when Empress Irini dragged me to Thessaloniki on a tour. She said she wanted to show Constantine his western border but I think she just wanted to personally lord it over the conquered Slavs. As far as I could see in the villages now on our side of that invisible line, those heathens didn't know or care where the new border was, they hated us all the same.

I refused to go to the Triumph that Irini gave Stavrakios in January, even though she summoned me by letter. I wrote on the back of her summons that the nuns were sick and I couldn't leave. Elias went. Afterwards, he sat in Father Dimitrios's cottage with me and Sister Matrona and Aspasia and spat out the news like it was curdled milk.

"Why she held a Triumph in January, no one knows," Elias said. "The campaign finished months ago and only a handful of half-frozen Slavs were shoved up Mesi Street which was ice and filthy slush all the way to the Hippodrome. People emptied their chamber pots out their windows but only a few people lined up to throw stones. I went to the Hippodrome and saw Constantine put his foot on the neck of a Slav officer before he was dragged off to the executioner. Our poor boy looked like he had lost the contents of his stomach."

No one was happy about that campaign, not even Stavrakios, so we heard when Constantine came out to Prinkypos in February. He loved early Lent on Prinkypos. It was still cold but a few red anemones dotted the south-facing slopes and tiny grape hyacinths poked their green stems up in the shade. Theo came with him, guarded by Aetios, that soulless eunuch whose gold chains around his neck grew thicker every time I saw him.

Megalo spotted the imperial yacht flying the imperial banner. When I got to the village, Elias had also arrived and was chatting with Constantine and Theo who were lounging on the bench against the church with Father Dimitrios. Constantine was thirteen then, taller than me, and so handsome with fair hair and a sweet smile. He rose and squeezed my arm. I missed his childhood embraces but his hand on my arm filled my heart with joy. Theo had brought sesame raisin cakes for the children and I swiped one as he handed them over. We watched Aetios drift down a lane, peering into open doorways.

Constantine scowled. "My mother sent that pig to spy on me. She trusts him more than she trusts me."

"May his bum be covered in boils," I cursed idly, munching on the sesame cake.

Theo nudged Constantine. "Tell her why we are here."

Constantine sighed gloomily. "My mother has been foraging in the Palace warehouses again. She says she has discovered the Chalke icon."

Father Dimitrios's dark eyes widened and he crossed himself. "The icon of Christ Pantokrator? Christ of the Chalke? The icon that your great-grandfather Emperor Leon tore off the arch of Chalke Gate? Riots broke out all over Constantinople!"

Theo nodded, as gloomy as Constantine. "Patriarch Pavlos swears it's the very icon, although how he knows, I have no idea. Is he so old that he can remember sixty years ago when icons were banned?"

Constantine made a face. "Nobody remembers what the Chalke icon looked like. I asked my advisors. Poor old Patriarch Pavlos will say anything my mother tells him. I suspect that my mother got Mihalis the Dragon to bring her an icon that he stole from one of the monasteries he burnt down."

"Why has Irini suddenly found this icon?" I demanded, suspiciously.

"She wants to plaster it back on Chalke Gate."

"Praised be to God!" Father Dimitrios lifted his clasped hands to the heavens.

Constantine's scowl deepened. "She is planning a procession to Holy Apostles Church. Priests will carry the icon on a bier. Patriarch Pavlos will conduct services. Then the procession will return to Chalke Gate and some monk will climb a ladder and plaster the icon back where it used to be."

Elias frowned. "Icons are still banned by edict. Chalke Gate is the entrance of the Great Palace. How can she plaster up an icon in such a public place?"

"She cannot," said Constantine emphatically. "It is a blatant denial of the edict. It constitutes actual heresy. But no-one has the courage to accuse my mother of heresy—certainly not Patriarch Pavlos."

"Then why is she doing this?" Father Dimitrios demanded.

"To show that she is Regent and she can do whatever she pleases. She sent Brother Grigorios out here to cover your convent church with icons and there wasn't a peep out of your bishop. Icons are appearing in churches across the Empire and Mihalis the Dragon isn't out there setting them on fire. But he will, I predict. The army vowed to Emperor Constantine in the name of God never to worship icons. To break a vow is to deny God—a crime punishable by excommunication or death. When my mother plasters that icon back over Chalke Gate, the army could well rise against her."

"Her risk is also yours, since you are Emperor," Elias noted with a frown.

"And she is risking the throne of the Isaurians," added Constantine soberly. "If the army arrests her, they will appoint some commander as Regent for me. He could decide to seize the throne for himself."

"Explain to me why she is mounting the icon on Chalke Gate, if it is such a risk." Father Dimitrios insisted.

"She believes the people and monks will love her and will be loyal to her if she gives them this icon. They never gave up their belief in icons. They just hid them. Monks kept painting them. She thinks the people and monks will stop the army from arresting her."

It came to me then, what Irini was doing. "She is putting the Chalke icon back up to test the reaction of the army. She wants to know what they will do if she convenes an ecumenical council to bring back icons."

Constantine grimaced. "She can't convene a council. Only an emperor can do that, not a regent. I told her. I also told her that I will wear the crown in five years and I will refuse to convene any such council. My father, my grandfather, and my great-grandfather all banned icons. Why would I change their decisions? Anyway, the monks and the people can't save her from the army. For that, she will have to rely on Stavrakios and Aetios and her many other eunuchs."

Theo nodded soberly. "Her eunuchs hold every major post in the Palace, including the Palace Guard. Aetios sleeps across her doorway, fully armed. The army will have to get past them."

"Which they will do gladly," Constantine said with a burst of enthusiasm. "They hate Stavrakios and Aetios. A rumour is going around that the two army officers who were captured by Harun along with Stavrakios were colluding with Tatzates and led Stavrakios into that trap. We are paying one hundred and sixty thousand gold nomismata a year to Harun al-Rashid, which the Treasury cannot afford. Last week in the Consistory, Nikiforos from the Finance Ministry told my mother that she needed to raise taxes to find the money. She did the opposite. She told the tax authorities to lower taxes. She wanted the love of the people. She would have more money if she hadn't squandered it on that Slav campaign," he added bitterly.

"Stavrakios took back our old borders," Father Dimitrios was protesting.

"The other commanders did the real soldiering," said Constantine. "Then Stavrakios complained that he didn't get enough booty. He demanded that my mother reward him with gold coins. Which she has done! Lavishly."

"The other commanders are furious," nodded Theo. "The kapelaria are full of angry soldiers."

Constantine lowered his voice. "Several army officers came to me secretly. They want me to enact an edict to put myself on the throne. They say the army will back me and so will most of the senators and patricians."

"You're only thirteen," Elias said, entering the conversation. "You have to have a regent until you're eighteen."

"The army officers said they would name one of their commanders as regent. The worry is that this commander might not step down when I am eighteen." His young face darkened and he dropped his voice to a low murmur, with a glance at the guards chatting in the plateia. "My mother could refuse to step down."

"She wouldn't do that!" Father Dimitrios protested.

"My mother wants to be Empress in her own right and she will do anything to achieve that," Constantine said bitterly. "Everyone knows the rumours about how my grandfather died. And my father. She won't stop there."

"Don't listen to rumours." Elias glanced at the yacht

captain who was chatting with the fishermen.

I looked at the oarsmen who were napping in the shady plateia and became suddenly suspicious. "Why are you here? It can't be just to tell us that Irini has discovered the Chalke icon."

Constantine sighed. "She wants you to walk in the procession holding up your icon."

"You have an icon?" Father Dimitrios exclaimed.

I was so stunned, I couldn't breathe. Only a few people knew that I had an icon. Elias knew, because he had seen my icon of Saint Thekla during our journey to Constantinople. Sister Matrona knew, because she and I lived at Saint Emmelia convent where everyone had icons. That's why Mihalis the Dragon had burnt it down. Abbess Pulkeria spotted it when I lived there. So had Princess Anthusa, who often stayed there. Constantine saw it when he was a child. Irini knew because I had pressed my icon into her hand when I was in prison, deranged from hunger and thirst and thinking she was Saint Thekla. Now Irini had told Theo—and who else? Stavrakios? Aetios?

I found my voice. "Icons are banned, no matter what Empress Irini says or does. I am the Abbess of an imperial convent. I cannot walk through the streets of Constantinople flaunting the edicts of two emperors in front of the icon-hating army and priests. They could cut off my ears and my tongue."

Theo nodded briskly. "I told Irini that it was too dangerous. I said you would refuse. But you have to tell her, yourself. You don't have a choice," he added gently.

He was right. The Empress could throw me in prison

for refusing to obey her. And worse, I had vowed in the name of God to do whatever she wanted. Resentment burned my throat.

Father Dimitrios looked at me sternly. "Abbess Thekla, God is calling you. Help the Regent bring back our icons."

On reluctant feet, I climbed to the convent and went into my study to take Saint Thekla from the secret drawer in my desk. The room glowed with the beautiful objects that Empress Irini had sent—hanging glass lamps, thick draperies, coloured glass windows. The nuns had woven cushions for the carved benches and chairs. The soft sounds of the convent calmed me. These gentle noises were my heart and soul. This was my home. If I didn't obey Empress Irini, I would lose both my icon and my home. I propped the tiny icon against my ink bottle and called Sister Matrona, Sister Evanthia, and Sister Efthia into my study. Aspasia followed, sensing trouble. Their eyes fell on my icon but they showed no surprise. I explained the situation.

"We all know you have an icon," said Sister Efthia, calmly. "The entire village knows, for heaven's sake. Many of the nuns have icons. I have an icon of Saint Efthia. It's time we brought them out."

"I agree," said Sister Evanthia.

"If Brother Grigorios can paint them on the walls of the church, we can bring ours out in the open," said Sister Matrona.

"But should I obey the Empress's order and carry Saint Thekla in the procession?" I asked them.

"Too dangerous," said Sister Evanthia, emphatically.

"Bringing our icons out in the safety of the convent is far different than carrying your icon in a procession for everyone to see."

"Surely the Empress knows you can't bring your icon out in public," frowned Sister Efthia.

Sister Matrona narrowed her eyes. "This isn't about your icon. She wants you in Constantinople for some other reason. You will have to go and find out."

Thoughtfully, I closed the door behind them and sat down at my desk. "Dear Saint Thekla," I said to her sweet face, "Should I carry you openly in the procession? I will be defying an imperial edict. You could be burnt and I could be thrown in prison. But if I refuse, Irini could send me into exile. Worse, I will be breaking my vow to obey her that I made before God." I closed my eyes and waited until I knew what to do.

Aetios kept his piggy eyes on me in the passenger cabin all the way to Constantinople. I wondered if Empress Irini had told him I had an icon. My anger started to build. Irini had said to me, "This will be our secret," when she had returned my icon to me. She had lied. I was still angry at her when we climbed the marble steps of Daphne Palace and entered her map room.

The Empress was lounging on a couch talking to Stavrakios who was sitting at the table looking over some pages of papyrus with Tarasios and Theodore. Irini was thirty-two that year and her beauty was staggering. She had tied back her glossy chestnut hair with a scarf twisted with a string of pearls. Theodore was only six years younger but he seemed older, a short, round man with flushed cheeks and a rushed manner of speaking.

"Thanks be to God who has brought Abbess Thekla safely to us," Theodore said pompously.

"Thanks be to the captain of the yacht," I muttered. Then my gaze fell upon a narrow table against the wall and the small wooden icon on a stand that nested within a wreath of rosemary boughs.

The icon was the size of my two hands. The image of Christ Pantokrator gazed at me, the same image that gazed from the ceiling of the Church of Holy Apostles. The icon glowed in the light of the small candle that flickered at its base. I couldn't take my eyes off it.

"Christ of the Chalke." Empress Irini announced with triumph. "It was hidden in an imperial warehouse."

"Because it was banned by imperial edict," pointed out Constantine in a cold voice. "It should have been burnt with the rest of the icons all over the Empire. You should burn it now. At least, put it back where it was hidden."

Empress Irini rose, bringing Tarasios and Theodore scrambling to their feet. "Everyone out except Abbess Thekla." When we were alone, she said, "Now tell me. Is this the real Chalke icon?"

I stared at her, confused. "I couldn't possibly say, Highness."

"Of course you can. That's why I sent for you. You have an icon; you know what they look like. Abbess Pulkeria very likely has icons hidden somewhere but she will pretend she cannot advise me on this one. Patriarch Pavlos says this is the real Chalke icon, but he tells me whatever I want to hear. You will tell me the truth. Is this the icon that was torn from the arch of Chalke Gate sixty years ago?"

I gazed at the bit of painted wood. A faded and chipped Christ gazed back at me. How could I possibly know if this was a real icon? Irini dropped onto a couch and accepted a cup of wine from the eunuch Nikitas.

"I was considering having it carried in procession to Holy Apostles and back to Chalke Gate. Or putting it on display in the Church of Holy Wisdom, like we do the Splinter of the True Cross. After a few days on view, bishops would carry it in procession from Holy Wisdom across the Augustaion to Chalke Gate. But then I realised that there will be people who remember real icons. The monks who are still painting them will get close enough to judge whether this is real or fake. The slightest whisper that it is false and I will lose credibility. People will laugh."

"Summon Father Dimitrios and Brother Grigorios," I stammered. "They know more about icons than I do."

She shook her head. "If I summon them, everyone will know that I have doubts. But I can summon you any time I want and no one thinks twice. Now look closely and tell me the truth. Real or fake?"

"Father Dimitrios says that wherever the saint's image is, there is the saint. But I don't know if every image of a saint is an icon."

"I don't care," she snapped. "Just tell me, is this the Christ of the Chalke?"

"You yourself once said that an icon is what you want it to be," I said.

Her voice grew hard. "Don't play games. Yes or no?"

Feeling confused and deeply afraid, I forced my reluctant feet closer to the bit of wood. Then, oddly, there came into my heart a kind of yearning. So I told her what she wanted to hear, like I always did, although lately it was getting harder and sometimes my tongue got away from me and I told her the truth.

"Yes, Highness, this is a real icon. Whether it is the original Chalke icon, I couldn't possibly know."

Relief flooded her smile. "Now I can plan the ceremony. Patriarch Pavlos claims that he is too weak to walk to Holy Apostles and back. And Stavrakios says that if I put it on display in Holy Wisdom, the army could snatch it and burn it. Tarasios says it is enough to have it carried in procession from the Great Palace across the Augustaion to the Church of Holy Wisdom for prayers, then back to Chalke Gate where it will be plastered on the arch. Until then, I'm keeping it here."

I accepted a glass of wine from Nikitas and took a strengthening gulp. "Highness, I cannot carry Saint Thekla in the procession."

Irini yawned. "Of course you can't. I only wanted you to tell me if this icon is real. I couldn't tell Theo or Constantine the real reason and I knew you wouldn't come if my demand wasn't urgent."

I laughed. What else could I do? I looked at the little icon glowing softly in the candlelight. I touched my fingers to my lips and lightly grazed the feet.

Empress Irini had gone over to the map of the Empire and was running her finger along a bright red line. "This is our new border with the Slavs, thanks to Stavrakios. I'm going there this summer for an official visit. Constantine and Theo will accompany me. And you."

Dismay flooded me even though I should have been used to her demands after years of being at her beck and call. "Empress, summer is the growing season. I need to supervise the nuns. Otherwise our harvest will not feed us through the winter."

She selected a pastry from a tray that Nikitas was holding out. "You will share my cabin as my personal guard. We will stay in Thessaloniki some days. It is our second largest city and I need to show my presence. I have commissioned a mosaic of Saint Dimitrios for the church to demonstrate my piety and philanthropy. Many empresses founded churches just to be called pious. Empress Verina is called 'The beloved of God' because of her non-stop church-building. Empress Theodora, the prostitute wife of Justinian, cleaned her reputation by building churches. You've seen the inscription in the Church of Saints Sergios and Bacchos: 'God-crowned Theodora, whose mind is adorned with piety, whose constant toil lies in efforts to nourish the destitute.'"

She returned her attention to the map. "We will visit Veria, fifty miles from Thessaloniki. Stavrakios destroyed it and I have ordered the army of Thrace to rebuild it. I am renaming it Irinopolis. It will be in a new theme which I am calling Makadonia. I will appoint new bishops."

Nikitas murmured in her ear. She smiled. "I have a visitor. Go talk to Constantine, Thekla. He will want to complain about me."

Constantine was pacing his room in a foul mood. "My mother tells me where to go, what to do, who to talk to!" he fumed, slamming his fist into the cushions. "She is making me walk in this procession to put the icon back on Chalke Gate. And then, instead of my military training on the frontier, I must go with her on this trip to Thessaloniki and watch her parade herself across the Empire. She is naming a town after herself! When I am eighteen, I will change the name back. And I will tear the Chalke icon off Chalke Gate. My father and my grandfather were right. The veneration of icons is nothing more than idol worship."

His words struck a chill in my heart. "From what I see, people do want their icons."

"That may be, but she is not doing it for the people. She is testing the waters for this ecumenical council she wants to stage. She wants to see what the army and the bishops will do if she plasters this icon on Chalke Gate."

The next morning, the eunuch Nikitas led Theo and me out Chalke Gate and across the Augustaion which was the broad walled area between the Great Palace and the Church of Holy Wisdom. Nikitas hammered on the door of the silk factory. It was locked, as were all businesses on a Sunday. Another of Irini's eunuchs opened the door only enough to let us in and led us up the stairs to the flat roof. Below us lay the broad Augustaion. I could see the red tile roof of Chalke Gate which was a square structure open on three sides and held up by pillars on the four corners. We lay down, hidden behind a low wall, and peered through the gaps. An excited crowd was filling the Augustaion. Soldiers were pushing people away from Chalke Gate, from the Patriarch's residence, the Patriarchal Library, and off the steps of the Church of Holy Wisdom. I spotted Abbess Pulkeria by the statue of Emperor Theodosius.

Finally, Chalke Gate opened and Palace eunuchs in their white tunicas bordered with purple unrolled a long red carpet across the Augustaion and up the steps of the Church of Holy Wisdom. Drums began beating and musicians marched out of Chalke Gate playing flutes and clashing cymbals. Behind them walked an acolyte carrying the tall gold cross with the Splinter of the Holy Cross embedded at the top. Hundreds of hands crossed breasts, like tall grass stirred by a breeze. Patriarch Pavlos stumbled out, his long white hair flowing from his tall red mitre. His pale face swung right and left like a human censor as he held up his age-mottled hands to bless the crowd.

Theo murmured, "Some bishops of Constantinople are accusing the Patriarch of being an idol worshipper because he is taking part in this ceremony. He is afraid of being poisoned. He has his meals sent from the Monastery of Floros where he used to be a monk."

Empress Irini and Constantine walked out together, the handsome, fair-haired, scowling young man and his beautiful, dark-haired, smiling mother. Sunlight flashed on their slender gold crowns and sliver robes. People dropped flat in full prostration.

Then came the Chalke icon. Four scarlet-robed bishops carried it, propped on a stand, on a bier draped in purple velvet. The crowd went so silent that I could hear the swish of hands crossing hearts and the soft murmur of prayers.

"Is this the real icon?" Theo whispered. "Or an invention of Irini's?"

"People believe what they want to believe," I replied,

my eyes on the people wiping away their tears, holding up their children.

The scarlet-robed bishops, richly-dressed patricians, and pompous senators shuffled into the Church of Holy Wisdom for prayers. I rolled onto my back and looked up into the cloudless blue sky. The thin, old man's voice of Patriarch Pavlos chanting the prayers floated out the door. Then the Palace guards were again shoving everyone off the red carpet to make way for the return procession. Irini and Constantine came first, then Patriarch Pavlos, who looked exhausted, then a red puddle of bishops gathered around Chalke Gate. A monk climbed up a ladder to the arch and slapped a trowel of wet plaster onto the marked spot. Patriarch Pavlos lifted the icon from the bier, kissed it, and handed it to a young monk who looked pale with nerves. He kissed it, carried it slowly up the ladder, then pressed it firmly into the plaster. A cheer rose up so suddenly that the monk took fright and nearly fell off the ladder, causing a ripple of laughter. Patriarch Pavlos did more chanting and it was over. Empress Irini and Constantine went through Chalke Gate into the Great Palace, the Patriarch and the bishops went into the Patriarchate, and the crowd left for the eateries. I caught up with Abbess Pulkeria who was resting with some nuns on the steps of the Milion.

"She's done it," I murmured, feeling oddly bewildered. "She told me that she would bring back icons and she has."

Abbess Pulkeria shook her head. "This is her first skirmish in a long war over icons. She cannot win it without allies and who does she have? Patriarch Pavlos is too old and weak to defy the edicts of previous emperors and the previous ecumenical council. Who else is there?" She looked at me, hard. "Be careful, my dear. You have vowed loyalty to Empress Irini but she has not vowed loyalty to you. If you are arrested for having an icon, she may not be able to help you. She may not even try. You will simply be another casualty in her war over icons."

Chapter VII

The journey to Thessaloniki by warship is pleasant if you are not seasick. I stood at the rail trying to quell my nausea by fastening my gaze on the green forests of Thrace. We dropped anchor for a night in the breathlessly hot port of Kallipolis at the top of the Dardanellia passage to the Aegean Sea. Slaves were moving cargo on and off merchant ships. That night, sweating in my bunk, I heard Empress Irini speak under her breath. Perhaps she thought I was sleeping. Perhaps her soul wanted her to release her memories. Her words were as soft as the splash of waves against our prow.

"The vomiting started before Thessaloniki. I thought I was ill, so I went willingly when Theo took me to the clinic of Doctor Moses in Thessaloniki while Emperor Constantine went off to tour the Bulgar border. Doctor Moses explained why I was vomiting and gave me a strong potion to make me sleep. I had no choice but to drink. When I awoke, it was over. I prayed for God to release my soul from my body but He didn't. Later, Theo took me to the Church of Saint Dimitrios and I begged the saint for death. Finally, the saint has answered my prayers. Emperor Constantine is dead. Leon is dead. And I sit on their throne."

I lay, unable to move, scarcely able to breathe. She said nothing more and finally I fell asleep.

The next day, we dropped anchor at Thessaloniki. I liked the town right away, the way the walls rose up from the sea and circled the town. The city gates opened into a wide plateia with the Church of Saint Dimitrios. We went inside, escorted by the mayor, the bishop, and every priest, monk, official, and rich citizen who could cram into the lovely cool church. Empress Irini seemed oddly nervous. Perhaps she was remembering when she was here last. Her nerves sharpened her cheekbones and deepened her dark eyes. People couldn't take their eyes off her.

My eyes were on the mosaics of Saint Dimitrios that covered the walls despite two generations of icon-destroying emperors. Perhaps those rulers had feared the wrath of Saint Dimitrios who was said to rise from his tomb when the Slavs attacked and frighten them off with terrible noises and smells.

Empress Irini and her attendants slept in the lavish home of the richest citizen and I lodged in a convent that served the worst supper I had ever choked down. The next day, I lied to the abbess that Empress Irini needed me to stand behind her at meals and taste her food. Empress Irini had a taster at the Great Palace, I told her, which was the truth. Then I ate at the local eateries, which served up excellent fare.

Some days later, we left for Irinopolis, riding on mules. Constantine rode in a gloomy silence. I could sympathise. We were riding through land that Stavrakios had wrested back from the Slavs and Irini had refused to let Constantine join the campaign. Theo wasn't speaking much either and neither was Irini so we rode in blessed silence. I hadn't been on a mule since I left my family home and I liked feeling the steady rhythmic sway through the deep quiet forest. I liked the heavy scent of moss and the calls of birds. I had never imagined mountains could rise so high.

Veria, now Irinopolis, sat by a wide river at the foot of a mountain. The town gates were smashed and the cottages inside were a shambles. A few people in filthy clothing watched us sullenly from a distance. We camped outside the walls and returned to Thessaloniki the next day. I was relieved to get back on our warship.

We were nearly home when a small imperial warship flagged us down. I was on deck with Theo looking at the ruins of the Anastasian Wall, which had been built by an early emperor seven miles from Constantinople as a first line of defence. The captain of the other vessel shouted that he needed to speak to Emperor Constantine and Regent Irini.

That day is seared into my memory— the trembling voice of the captain, the seamen and guards crossing themselves and Theo's long sceptical look at Irini.

"Highnesses," said the captain, standing stiffly at attention, "Some peasants were stealing stones from the Anastasian Wall and they have uncovered a wooden coffin. There are words scratched on it plain to see.

The words speak of the coming of Christ and also of Constantine and Irini. A local monk has pronounced it a miracle."

Empress Irini crossed herself and announced that we must bear witness to this miracle. A mule was found for her and the rest of us stumbled through the grasslands, following the falling-down Anastasian Wall which stretched as far as the eye could see. The miracle site was clogged with peasants and monks on their knees before a tall mound of wildflowers. Our guards shoved everyone roughly aside and a monk shifted the flowers. Underneath was a jumble of broken planks that at one time might possibly have been a small coffin. I could only make out a few letters scratched into the wood, but Empress Irini dropped to her knees and read aloud in a high clear voice.

"'Christ will be born of the Virgin Mary and I believe in Him. O Sun, you will see me again in the reign of Constantine and Irini.'"

She then rose and addressed the crowd of gawkers in a voice that rang like a bell. "Good people, devoted Christians. We have before us a simple coffin placed here by a prophet who inscribed these words upon it long before the time of Christ. His message is clear. He has predicted the coming of Christ and also the reign of myself and my son Constantine. This is indeed a miracle! Praised be to God!"

Theo crossed himself piously but his hand remained over his mouth to hide his murmur to Constantine, "The miracle is that those bits of wood survived since before Christ!"

Constantine was covering his mouth to conceal his laughter.

The monks hoisted the coffin onto a cart they had taken from a peasant and dragged it to our vessel. News of the miracle coffin somehow had preceded us and fishing boats crowded the waters around the Palace harbour gates. People stood on the sea wall in such numbers that the real miracle was that no one fell into the sea. Empress Irini stood on deck where all could see her, clasping her hands over her heart as she watched the tumble-down coffin be transferred carefully onto the imperial yacht. Later I learned that it was taken up the Golden Horn to the Church of Blachernae where Patriarch Pavlos prayed over it.

I did not follow Irini and Constantine up the steep steps to Daphne Palace. Rather, I mounted the winding lanes to Ta Gastria convent where Abbess Pulkeria greeted me kindly and said she had a guest room available. We sat in her study and she refilled my little glass of elderberry wine several times while I related my account of the journey and the miracle coffin.

She shook her head. "Such foolishness. The Empress thinks she can fool people. She is creating a legend for herself, I suppose, like Empress Theodora. It won't be long before she goes too far."

"If she hasn't already." I slept well that night, secure inside the Ta Gastria convent walls and the sensible embrace of Abbess Pulkeria's words. The next morning, I got the early boat to Chalkidon and walked the twenty miles to Pendykion, arriving as Elias was going into the kapelarion for supper.

"Cousin!" he greeted me for the benefit of the towns-people, and ordered up sea bass stuffed with greens. He listened intently as I ate greedily and told him of the miracle coffin.

"How foolish does she think we are?" he muttered.

"No-one will deny the miracle," I pointed out.

He was curious about Constantine's reaction to the miracle and was still asking questions about the miracle when I fell asleep in his arms.

The prayer that Patriarch Pavlos chanted over the miracle coffin and its strange inscription was his last act as Patriarch. Elias brought the news of his flight a few weeks later, when Constantine and Irini were on Prinkypos. I had left Irini enjoying the autumn sun in the garden while I went down to the village with Aspasia to buy fish. We were chatting with Father Dimitrios and Constantine when Elias sailed in and handed Constantine a rolled up papyrus addressed to Empress Irini.

"I'm the Emperor; this should be addressed to me," he snarled, and cracked open the seal. He skimmed it and his anger changed to astonishment. "Patriarch Pavlos has fled the Patriarchate without a word to anyone. He is now at the Monastery of the Floros wearing the robes of a monk!"

Father Dimitrios shook his head sadly. "May God give him strength."

"That poor, suffering old man." Constantine put down the letter and gazed sadly at the sun-sparkled sea. "My father treated him poorly, which was unlike him. He knew that Pavlos believed in the sanctity of icons be-cause Pavlos had told my father that he could not lead the Church if he had to stand beside an Emperor who wanted icons banned. My father appointed him Patriarch anyway, then made him vow to condemn icons in front of everyone in the Church of Holy Wisdom. His first official act was to bury my father. Then my mother forced him to talk me through ordaining my two uncles as priests on the Day of Nativity, and then talk them through giving the Eucharist. I was nine but I remember the day clearly. I thought he would collapse in shame."

Constantine's sensitive mouth twisted. "After that, my mother made him return the Chalke icon to Chalke Gate. Many bishops were whispering that he was an idol worshipper. Finally, he had to carry out a service over that strange coffin that my mother found by the Anastasian Wall."

Elias then surprised me. "I tried to persuade Leon not to name Pavlos as Patriarch," he said. "Then I begged him not to force the old man to forswear his beliefs. I think it was the first time that Leon had ever made an independent decision and he didn't want to back down."

I stared at him. Years before, I had learned that Elias and Leon had been childhood friends but I was astonished at this degree of intimacy. Constantine didn't seem surprised.

"I'm surprised Patriarch Pavlos didn't flee the Patriarchate before now," he said. "Or die."

Constantine took the letter to Irini who was resting in the shade of the grape arbour. I brought out some cool mint tea.

"Patriarchs come and patriarchs go," she yawned, swatting away a wasp with the letter. "Constantine, we must go visit the poor man so he can explain himself before I announce that he has retired. Then I must name a new patriarch. Thekla, you will come with us. I want you to visit Evdokia and find out what she is plotting. And you can come with us to the Monastery of the Floros. It is one of those small exquisite monasteries built by incredibly rich people to store their ossuaries. Emperor Constantine tried to have it shut down for refusing to obey his ban on icons. He failed, somehow."

Irini wrote a message for Stavrakios to send the yacht for her and I took it down to Elias. He was preparing to leave. He slid the letter into his pouch.

"What is she planning?" he demanded.

"She is making me visit Evdokia at her convent to find out what she is plotting. And I must go with Irini and Constantine to visit Patriarch Pavlos and ask why he is resigning."

"Poor old Pavlos," he said, shaking his head. "His retirement won't last long."

"What do you mean?" I demanded, but he pushed off without answering.

The next morning, we boarded the yacht and that very evening went to visit Patriarch Pavlos at the Floros monastery. Monks carried him into the courtyard in a chair. The September day was warm but he clutched a heavy wool shawl around his thin shoulders. He had to stop for breath every few words.

"These years that I have served as Patriarch have been a burden on my soul," he rasped with bowed head. "I regret the schism between Constantinople and the Latin church over icons. I repent giving support to the heresy condemning icons. I regret the vow I made to Emperor Leon. I beg to resign."

Empress Irini responded with an encouraging smile. "Patriarch Pavlos, neither Constantine nor I have enforced the ban on icons. You yourself restored the icon of Christ Pantokrator to Chalke Gate. The mosaics of Saint Dimitrios remain in his church in Thessaloniki and I have commissioned another. There is no reason for you to resign because of the ban on icons."

A sheen of sweat covered the Patriarch's pale face. "My health cannot allow me. I beg you, find a man who can lead the Church in legally restoring icons."

"Can you name a man capable of this feat?" she inquired sweetly.

"Consul Tarasios. He is the only man," he gasped.

I was stunned. Tarasios? The Palace administrator? I felt Constantine stiffen. He glared at his mother but he held his tongue until we were inside the coach and returning to the Palace.

"You forced poor old Pavlos to resign, didn't you?" he raged at her. "You told him to recommend Tarasios."

Empress Irini smiled. "Tarasios is an excellent choice. We will summon him and start the process of making him Ecumenical Patriarch of Constantinople."

"But Tarasios isn't a bishop. He isn't even a monk!" Constantine shouted. "He is a Palace administrator! You can't name a secular pen-pusher as ecumenical patriarch!"

Empress Irini remained calm. "A good administrator is precisely what the Church needs. Tarasios comes from generations of Palace administrators. His father was a high-ranking official and patrikios. Tarasios himself has risen to seventh highest in the Ministry of Finance. He is a senior court dignitary at the level of generals and governors. If anyone can make the Church run smoothly, he can."

"But he's not clergy! He's a layman!"

Empress Irini shrugged. "I will find a priest to ordain him. Dino, listen to me: Tarasios is the best choice because he is not beholden to anyone in the Church hierarchy. He owes no-one so he cannot be influenced or controlled. And he is certainly devout; he has built himself a monastery."

"I have been to this monastery!" shouted Constantine. "He built it to hide his wealth so it cannot be taxed. The land is worked by monks for free."

"I'm not discussing this any further. Thekla, I'm letting you out here. Go to the convent where Evdokia is living. Tell me if she is still alive and what she is plotting."

The former Empress Evdokia was sitting under the kitron tree in the narrow courtyard when the novice let me in. I thought she would order me away, but she pointed at a bench with her fan. "What does that pagan want?" she demanded, as I settled myself gratefully.

"The Empress is concerned about your health," I murmured.

She laughed. "You are as great a liar as she. I hear Patriarch Pavlos has escaped her clutches. Is this true?"

"The Patriarch has retired to his monastery."

"More power to him, although she won't let him live long. I'm surprised that I'm still alive, myself, although I suppose it's because I have no money or power. Who is she naming to replace him?"

I had expected disbelief when I told her, but she merely pursed her lips, thinking. "She wants to bring back icons, obviously. That's why she plastered back the Chalke Gate icon. Tarasios can do it; it's a path to more power, which he likes. He can go about it however he likes since he bows to no-one in the Church hierarchy. Or the Palace. He knows too much about people. He and Nikiforos in the Ministry of Finance are as thick as thieves."

"Nikiforos the Accountant?" I was confused.

She nodded absently, her thoughts moving on. "Irini thinks my husband fell under her spell. He didn't. She had started to annoy him with her demands for money. I told him to send her back to Athens but he let her stay. I supposed she was still good company, despite her strong-willed ways. She was quick-witted and had that beautiful face and body. He underestimated her, as did I. She wants to be Empress in her own right. She won't succeed. Tell her that from me. Tell her to let Constantine be crowned and be satisfied with being the mother of the Emperor. No man in the army or the Church or the Palace will kneel to a woman alone on the throne."

I passed her words on to Irini, the last part. She laughed and told me to go and get Constantine out of his foul mood.

Constantine was still sulking. He sent a eunuch for our supper. "Tarasios wants power," he fumed, pacing his room. "He doesn't care that he has no experience in Church affairs and no qualifications to lead the Church. His only qualification is that he will do whatever my mother wants."

I spoke cautiously. I was starting to understand Empress Irini's reasoning. "Dino, your mother wants to restore icons into common use and she thinks Tarasios has the administrative ability to make this happen. And he's a man; a woman can't lead the Church. People are eager to have their icons. You saw the crowds when she put the Chalke icon back over Chalke Gate."

Constantine's voice grew hard. "My mother doesn't care about icons or what the people want. She wants the throne and she thinks that giving the people back their icons will get it for her. She is wrong. The army decides who to raise on their shields as emperor and they won't raise a woman." His voice dropped and became low and intense with fury. "When I am eighteen and wear the crown, I will arrest my mother and lock her in that dungeon under your convent on Prinkypos!"

I understood his anger and frustration. His mother was keeping him from taking his role as Emperor, as much he could before he was crowned at eighteen. At that moment, the veil of time lifted for me and I saw into the future. A war was coming between these two people to whom I had given my loyalty and my heart, and I would be caught in the middle.

The next morning, I took the ferry to Chalkidon, tired from my distress in mind and body. When I stepped off the ferry in Chalkidon, I went inside a convent for a moment of peace before walking to Pendykion. An icon of Saint Ekaterini graced an icon stand in the vestibule. I kissed her feet and crossed myself, then made a mental note to have Brother Grigorios paint her on a pillar in our convent church. I lit a candle and stuck it in the sand pit, not sure whether to pray for Irini's soul first or Constantine's. It was not the last time I had to make that choice.

A farmer let me ride to Pendykion in his empty wagon and I arrived as Elias was talking to a tired-looking mail courier. Elias and I shared a pot of rabbit stew in the kapelarion. "Patriarch Pavlos has died," he said. "I just got the news."

I crossed myself, not surprised. "Emperor Leon forced the poor man to disavow his belief in icons. His shame and grief killed him."

"More likely, he ate something that disagreed with him," Elias said darkly, stabbing his knife into a rabbit thigh. "I wonder which poor cleric the Empress will name as our next patriarch."

"Tarasios." I gnawed on a rabbit thigh bone.

Elias put down his knife and stared at me. "The Palace administrator? Consul Tarasios? You must have the wrong name."

"I have the right name," I said irritably. "Irini thinks that Tarasios can help her bring back icons."

Elias shook his head decisively. "She's mad. A council of bishops must be called to bring back icons. They must vote to revoke the ban. They won't. If they did, every bishop and priest who has enforced the ban over the last sixty years will be accused of heresy. The punishment is death or exile."

I sucked the marrow out of the bone. "Irini will achieve it. No one helped her when Emperor Leon shouted that he would never again share her bed. Now he is dead and she is Empress."

He narrowed his eyes. "Constantine said that she wants to be Empress in her own right. Does she actually believe that giving the people back their icons will achieve this?"

I picked up another rabbit bone and nodded.

He shook his head. "If Tarasios doesn't achieve that for her, I hope he has a good food taster."

A few days before the Feast of Nativity, Constantine came out to Prinkypos with Theo. We sat in Father Dimitrios's cottage with Brother Grigorios, warming ourselves by the goat-dung fire. Father Dimitrios had four children by now and they watched wide-eyed as Constantine ranted with bitter anger about his mother.

"Tarasios is being ordained this very day. He will give the Eucharist and be a priest."

"That was fast!" Father Dimitrios exclaimed.

Constantine nodded, grimly. "My mother called a lot of patricians and wealthy people to Magnavra Palace. She made me stand beside her while she introduced Tarasios as a candidate for Ecumenical Patriarch of Constantinople. Tarasios spoke—and a lovely, humble speech it was," he added sarcastically. "He confessed that he had struggled with doubts about accepting the honour. He admitted that his life had been spent on secular matters and he would wear the mitre only if my mother and I would convene an ecumenical council to bring about unity within the Church. He promised he would obey the edicts of the six previous Ecumenical Councils—not the last one when they banned icons— and icons would be restored. He was approved in the first show of hands. My mother had planted the votes, of course," he added sourly.

"Does Tarasios have any allies in the Church?" Father Dimitrios asked. "Rising in the Church hierarchy depends on having other bishops behind you."

Theo nodded. "Tarasios neatly took care of that. He announced that everyone present must swear loyalty to him to make certain that he was following the will of the people. Of course they did. Irini will appoint him as Ecumenical Patriarch on the Day of Nativity."

Constantine looked at me. "I want you to come back with me today, Auntie Thekla. You can keep me from shouting at her."

I nodded but with a heavy heart. I would miss watching Father Dimitrios bless the fishing boats with the holy smoke from his censor. I would miss hearing him chant the Nativity liturgy in the church by the harbour. I would miss joining the village families for the Nativity meal. I put Sister Matrona in charge and reluctantly followed Theo and Constantine onto the yacht.

Empress Irini was in her map room surveying a display of tapestries spread out by some merchants when Constantine and I entered. She had started colouring her hair with henna, I noticed. I wondered if my hair was also going silver. We had no mirrors in the convent except for a silver tray that was going black. Irini pointed at a tapestry so finely woven with such brilliant colours that the figures seemed to move. "I'll have that one. Nikitas, pay them for it," she ordered, and the eunuch quickly ushered the merchants out.

Irini pointed at a papyrus on the table. "Constantine,

read my letter to Pope Adrianos and tell me if it is clear. Tarasios has written to him and announced his appointment. He has also written to the Patriarchs of Jerusalem, Antioch, and Alexandria. My letter is my next move towards convening an ecumenical council." She reached for a pastry.

Constantine slumped on a couch to read. Part-way through, he put it down and spoke slowly and precisely. "You are inviting Pope Adrianos to an ecumenical council to be held in a year and a half. You are requesting his advice and assistance. You can't be serious."

"I'm serious about the council but not about his advice," she smiled. "I want the old goat to believe that he is organising this council. Then he will send his delegates and stop writing me letters objecting to Tarasios's rapid rise from layman to Patriarch. Read the rest." She selected another pastry.

Constantine took his time reading while Theo poked up the fire and I bolted down the rest of the pastries. Constantine put down the letter.

"You tell the Pope that the traditions of the Eastern Church have been corrupted by errors in dogma and interpretation of scripture. You say that you forced Patriarch Pavlos to resign because he was corrupted by this. You say that Tarasios believes in the true dogma of the combined Eastern and Western churches. It's a pack of lies and the Pope knows it. Why bother?"

"Because the Pope wants icons restored and this letter says we will do that, although not in so many words. This letter also promises that the bishops and priests who obeyed the ban on icons will not be accused of heresy and neither will our past three emperors. If Pope Adrianos agrees to all this, then I will have no further trouble with him."

Constantine tossed the pages onto the table. "The army will fight against bringing back icons because they took a vow to my grandfather not to revere them. The priests of Constantinople will fight this because they believe that they will be accused of heresy for obeying the edict banning icons all their lives. The senators and patricians and other dignitaries who obeyed the ban will fight it for the same reason. And they all won't like me because they will think that I am with you on this. Which I am not."

Empress Irini dusted the crumbs from her fingers. "My spies in Rome tell me that Pope Adrianos is considering allowing King Charles of the Franks to travel through the papal lands and invade our lands in Sicily and Calabria. The Pope is trying to frighten me so that I will give up the marriage to Rotrud. When he gets the letter that you have just read, he will approve the marriage."

"Don't be silly, Mother," Constantine scoffed. "Charles will invade Calabria and Sicily whenever he feels like it. My big question is, can you be sure of Tarasios? He could organize this council for you and when the army rises against you, not lift a finger to help you."

My pleasure at hearing him be strong in his opinion disappeared under my shock at Irini's response. "Tarasios will do what I tell him," she snapped. "He knows I will get rid of him just as I got rid of the two patriarchs before him."

I went with Constantine to his chambers. "What a

mess," he said gloomily, throwing himself on the couch. "I am betrothed to a girl whose father is preparing to invade our lands in Sicily and Calabria. I write to this female in Greek; she writes back in a mixture of Latin and German. She refers to God a great deal and seems to spend all her time on her knees in prayer. Happily, I will be in her presence only long enough to create an heir. I will be in court with King Charles, learning his manner of governing for when I am King of the Franks."

"Do you really think your mother will actually convene this council?"

He shook his head. "My mother can try to call together her tame bishops and priests and monks and pass a resolution to bring back icons. But the army is against it and so are most of the priests of Constantinople. They will do everything they can to block this. And if my mother succeeds, in five years when I am Emperor, I will convene another council and I will order them to ban icons, just as my grandfather did."

I marvelled at how well Dino understood the situation and his grasp of the power factions in the Empire. He should. He was thirteen, old enough to see battle, and he had been tutored in affairs of state since he was nine. What disturbed me, however, was his determination to ban icons.

"Do you want to ban icons because you truly believe they are idols that people would worship, like the Golden Calf? Or are you angry at your mother for keeping you from your duties as Emperor and combatting icons to fight her?"

His face darkened with anger and he looked much

older. "Yes, I blame my mother for keeping me from making the decisions that I could be making now. As for icons, they were banned by my father, my grandfather, and my great-grandfather. Why would I deny their wisdom?" He lowered his voice to a near whisper and his words chilled my heart. "Have you ever wondered at how quickly Patriarch Nikitas died after he told my mother that she could be divorced for not producing more children? Have you ever wondered at how quickly Patriarch Pavlos died after he recommended Tarasios as the next Patriarch? If he had lived longer and regained his strength, he might have publicly recanted his words."

I had to nod. The thought had occurred to me.

He lowered his voice even further. "Tarasios should watch his back."

On the Day of Nativity, I watched the newly ordained Tarasios kneel before Emperor Constantine and Empress Irini in the Church of Holy Wisdom and receive the tall mitre of patriarch on his head from her hands. Abbess Pulkeria and several nuns were resting on the steps of the Milion when I came out. I walked with them to Ta Gastria Convent to spend the night. The Abbess and I sat in her study and drank elderberry wine while I described the letter that Empress Irini had written to Pope Adrianos. She listened intently.

"Empress Irini is committing a rash act, elevating Tarasios to patriarch. He has not learned the ways of the Church from the inside and he has reached the pinnacle of Church authority without the support of the bishops. They will make him pay for this—and Empress Irini as well."

Morning came with bitter cold and a sky dark with clouds. I had turned down Constantine's offer to take the imperial yacht back to Prinkypos because I wanted to see Elias. I wanted him to quell the fear that was rising inside me, that Irini was taking a wrong path and she would drag Constantine down with her. I took the early ferry to Chalkidon with some monks and nuns who had watched Patriarch Tarasios receive the mitre. Their excited chatter made me ill. In Chalkidon, I got the last seat on the mail coach to Pendykion. Snow was drifting down as we pulled up at the Pendykion postal way-station. I nodded to Elias when he came out to unload the mail pouches, and continued to his rooms where I buried myself under his quilts. I slept, exhausted from the cold journey and the fights between Constantine and Irini. Elias brought a pot of venison stew and we ate in bed, wrapped in blankets, while I told him all I knew. He had no comfort to offer me except for his arms, where I slept the uneasy sleep of the innocent bystander.

***

Pope Adrianos accepted Irini's invitation to her council during early Lent. Irini and Constantine were on Prinkypos when Elias arrived with the mail. Constantine and I happened to be at the harbour and we brought the letter up to Irini who was sitting by the fire in my study. Constantine could now only enter the courtyard and my study at his age. He had turned fourteen in January and was settling into his character, a quiet, thoughtful young man. He watched his mother with no expression while she crowed over her success.

"The Pope will send delegates to my council," Irini

beamed, waving the letter. "He congratulates me on following his advice to restore icons. As if the council was his idea, the arrogant ass. He agrees no emperor will be judged a heretic for having banned icons, and no clergy will be called heretics for having obeyed or enforced the ban."

She read on and her eyes darkened in anger. "But the old goat demands that Eastern Orthodoxy recognise the primacy of Rome! He is mad! Does he believe that we are sheep gone astray who must return to the fold? I will never agree to this absurdity. Not only that, he demands that I return the papal sees of Illyricum to his authority!"

"Illyricum? Where is this?" I asked.

Constantine got up and pointed on the huge parchment map of the Empire of the Romans of the East that Irini had brought so many years before. "Illyricum is this tiny principality across the Adriatic Sea from Venice. It used to be under the jurisdiction of the Church of Rome. My grandfather took it under the Eastern Church. The Pope wants it back."

"Papal arrogance!" Empress Irini fumed.

"A game, Mama," Constantine countered, patiently. "You offer something, he offers something else, you both compromise. You want him to stop threatening our lands in Calabria and Sicily? Give the old goat back his Illyricum. What do we need it for anyway? It's too far away to send warships to protect it."

She stared moodily out the long windows to the courtyard where tiny grape hyacinths filled the flower beds. "I am having second thoughts about inviting those papists to my Council. Or monks, either. The Council will be in a year and three months, and already they are writing what they want discussed. It is not their Council! It is mine!"

"Maybe they have some good ideas," Constantine noted sarcastically.

"I make the agenda and no monk, priest, or papist is going to change it." She picked up another letter and scanned it, then threw it down. "I have ordered new coins to be minted to celebrate my Council. The idiot Master of the Mint tells me that a regent's image cannot go on a coin, that the images must be Constantine and his father. There's nothing I can do now. But this won't happen again."

She ran her fingers through her thick chestnut hair. "The Caliph is another annoyance. I announced at a meeting in the Consistory that I am not paying the Thief of Baghdad any more tribute for the peace we negotiated two years ago. It was not a military defeat; Tatzates turned traitor and lured Stavrakios into a trap. Why should I pay for entrapment?"

Constantine was patient. "Because, Mama, Caliph al-Mahdi will invade if we stop paying. We have had two years of peace. Let's keep it."

"If he invades, we will send him packing. Our armies are at full strength and our granaries are full. We can stop draining the Treasury with this tribute nonsense. I wrote to Mihalis the Dragon that I want him to launch a campaign against the Caliph this coming spring. I want him to attack Adata just over the border. Six years ago, the Dragon burnt it but the Caliph has rebuilt it into a stronghold for launching their attacks against us. I want it razed to the ground. For once, the Dragon agrees with me."

"Mistake!" Constantine exploded. "Do you not remember the advice my grandfather gave you? He said that we cannot afford to lose even one soldier. He kept our borders safe by fighting defensive wars—not crossing an enemy's borders and attacking their stronghold. We will gain nothing and lose many lives. Some of the Caliph's soldiers enlist just for the honour of dying." He dragged himself to his feet and went out.

Irini sighed. "I am tired of fighting with that child. And I'm tired of the whispers and gossip that infest the Palace. Remember, years ago before Dino was born, I showed you a place above Eleftherios Harbour where I wanted to build a palace of my own, where I could escape the Great Palace. I have told the Master Builder to draw up plans. I will call it Eleftherios Palace because the word means both 'not married' and 'free'. Finally, I am both."

It wasn't freedom that she wanted. It was power.

Chapter VIII

Irini left after a week but Constantine stayed on Prinky-pos until Holy Week. "My mother shuts me out of the planning meetings for her wretched council," he fumed. "The whole Palace is sniggering at me. She spends all day with Patriarch Tarasios and Theodore and Fanis, that hypocrite monk who sent Megalo out here to be a nun instead of giving her a divorce. They tell me nothing of what they are planning. My eunuchs have found out that this meeting will be at the Church of Holy Apostles in August. The month before that, she is planning another trip to Thessaloniki and she is making me go along. She knows that if I stay in Constantinople, I will try to stop this."

"She believes people want their icons back," I said, feebly.

"She isn't doing it for that reason," he protested, as he had before. "She is using it to get power. She also dreams that the council will cause Pope Adrianos to approve my marriage to Rotrud and stop Charles of the Franks from invading our lands in Calabria and Sicily. Wishful thinking! She is making enemies of the soldiers, senators, and priests—everyone except the monks, and they cannot keep her on the throne. I have no enemies in the priests or the senators, and the army will do what I say. I want to be crowned Emperor, right now, but Theo says I'm too young. You will come to this meeting in August. You can watch this disaster of my mother's and then you will understand why I should be crowned Emperor now."

So, in the hottest month of the year, Aspasia and I left the cool breezes of Prinkypos Island and went by a fisherman's boat to Pendykion where Elias put us on a coach packed with unwashed monks and priests. We covered our mouths and noses with our scarves to block the stench of sweat and foul breath. The road was dense with dark clerical bodies striding towards Constantinople. At Chalkidon, we jostled ourselves onto a ferry and climbed off into packs of clergy pushing through the narrow pedestrian passage of the Golden Gate. Mesi Street was as hot as an oven and clogged with priests shouting, "Stop the Council! Against God!" Monks were shouting back, "Bring back our holy icons!"

Aspasia went to stay with her sister and I continued to Chalke Gate where I arrived at the same time as Theo who was red-faced and dripping with sweat. The guards squeezed us through a barely opened gate. At Daphne Palace, I turned towards the bathhouse, desperate to get into clean clothes, but Theo jerked his head towards Daphne Palace and Irini's chambers. His tense, brusque manner, so unlike his usual relaxed charm, stilled my protest.

Irini was in her map room with Patriarch Tarasios, Brother Fanis, and Theodore who was twenty-eight and still had his cherubic cheeks and mouth that never stopped talking. He held a high-level Palace administrative position. Theo cut him off.

"Trouble," Theo said grimly. "The streets of Constantinople are seething with protestors."

Empress Irini was looking cool and pleased with herself in a green silk tunica, full silk trousers tight at the ankles, and jewelled sandals. She waved that away. "I have dealt with them. I have banned public protest."

"They didn't get the message," he snapped. "You have no idea of the strength of your opposition. The bishops of Constantinople are protesting as a group—the same bishops who came to you as a group and tried to get you to abandon this. I heard a rumour that they have conspired with the Palace Guard to break it up with force!" He raised his voice in frustration. "Why didn't you come back from Thessaloniki sooner? Why didn't you at least try to compromise with them. Now you and Constantine are in serious danger. Call this off, I beg you, Cousin. Make peace with those priests. Convene another council, later."

"No," snapped Irini, flatly. "I would lose all credibility. No one would return for another council."

Theodore nodded in his annoyingly pompous way. "I thoroughly agree. Hundreds of priests and monks have walked here from all over the Empire. The papal delegates have arrived from Rome. The delegates from the Patriarchates of Antioch and Jerusalem and Alexandria have risked their lives traveling through the Caliphate.

It's vital that we go on as planned."

"See?" Irini smiled triumphantly. "I can't let these brave clergy down."

Theo threw up his hands, exasperated. "Irini, most of them came here to vote against icons. They have obeyed the ban their entire lives and they are terrified that they will be called heretics and put to death! At best, they will lose their bishoprics and become paupers!"

Patriarch Tarasios shook his head. "Pope Adrianos has agreed with us that no clergy will be accused of heresy. His letter is right here."

"A letter! Who will believe a letter?" Theo exclaimed. He and Constantine stomped out of the room.

I crept out and went to Constantine's chambers. Theo was staring moodily out the window at the sea. Constantine put his arms around me like he hadn't done since he was a child. "She is pushing the Empire into civil war just to become Empress in her own right," he muttered with tears in his eyes.

"We still have to protect her," said Theo, not turning from the window. "Pray that none of us dies in the attempt."

The next morning, Theo and I went early to the Church of Holy Apostles to look at the situation, taking the back streets to avoid the noisy, belligerent protestors shouting, "Stop the Council! Against God!"

"They seem strangely bulky under their robes," Theo noted with a worried frown. We slipped through a narrow door at the back of the church after Theo showed the guard a letter that he obviously couldn't read, and gave him a silver coin. Grateful to be out of the roasting sun, we climbed to the balcony. The vast church spread out below us, filling up with chatting delegates.

Some tough-looking hooded monks with suspicious bulges under their tunicas were loitering near the red marble tomb of Constantine the Great. I spotted Theodore chatting up some papal legates in their dark robes. Theodore was wearing an undyed linen tunica that could have been a monk's robe but wasn't. That was Theodore: glib, eloquent, and neither clerk nor cleric. He began talking to Brother Fanis. I glared at him on Megalo's behalf. The balcony was filling up with monks. Monks are not known for their cleanliness and these hadn't bathed in weeks, if ever. Incense smoke thickened the air and made the stink worse. I held my scarf over my mouth and nose. A eunuch at the entrance hammered his staff on the marble floor sending echoes through the church.

"Here we go," said Theo, chewing on his thumbnail with worry.

Guards started efficiently clearing the central aisle by roughly shoving aside bishops, priests, abbots, and monks still greeting friends. Patriarch Tarasios began his measured tread down the aisle. I didn't like the man but I had to admire his courage. Despite the shouting from protesters outside and his packed and smelly surroundings, he wore his red brocade robes as if they had graced his thin shoulders for years, not months. Constantine and Irini walked behind him. Candlelight flashed on their robes embroidered in silver and gold thread. Jewels sparkled in their slender gold crowns. When they were seated, Patriarch Tarasios called everyone to prayer. Then he launched into his speech. Quickly, I detected

Theodore's eloquent style in the flow of his rolling, melodious near-chant.

"Today we are fulfilling the promise of Emperor Constantine and Empress Irini to restore the Constantinopolitan Patriarchate to its former elevated position in the eyes of our Christian neighbours. The misunderstandings of previous years are behind us. Today we will integrate Constantinople back into the wider Church."

Low murmurs rose but he kept going. He said that no previous emperor would be blamed for banning icons, but that the edicts forbidding the veneration of icons would be overturned. That's as far as he got.

Responding to some signal, monks and priests flung off their robes, revealing the uniforms of the Palace Guard and army. They began shouting, "Shut down the Council!" Bishops and priests joined in and the church thundered with a terrifying uproar of shouts and echoes. Theo pushed me down on the floor and drew his short sword.

"I'm going to help Irini and Constantine."

I peeked over the railing. Irini and Patriarch Tarasios had retreated into a corner with the few bishops who had helped organize the Council. Constantine and Irini's personal guards were holding off the mob with their short swords and daggers. I saw Theo struggling through the crowd beside Elias, knocking bodies aside to reach Irini and Constantine. Swords clashed, monks punched priests, bishops hit each other.

Suddenly, Stavrakios and Aetios stood in the doorway with the other eunuchs from Irini's household staff. With a shout, they drew their swords. The attackers backed off and Irini, Constantine, Patriarch Tarasios and the pro-icon bishops were hustled out. Someone bellowed, "We have won! The Council is abandoned!"

Cries of triumph echoed through the church and within minutes, it was empty. I hurried down the steps and stumbled over Theodore who was crawling out of an alcove under the stairs and holding his hand over a bruised cheek. I got him on his feet, skirted the jubilant protestors celebrating outside, and led him through back streets to Chalke Gate. I didn't see Elias anywhere. The guards hustled us inside.

Everyone was in the map room. Constantine was scowling by the window, arms crossed. Patriarch Tarasios and Brother Fanis were slumped on a couch. A sweaty and dishevelled Theo sat on the floor, leaning his head against the wall. Empress Irini was pacing in fury.

"I want names!" she shouted. "Tell me who started this riot and they will rot in prison!"

Constantine pointed a shaking finger at his mother. "You started it!" he shouted. "Theo and I warned you there would be trouble. Theo told you to delay this Council. How many bishops had to come here and tell you they intended to honour the ban on icons before you believed them? What happened today is all your fault!"

Theo backed him up, more angry than I had ever seen him. "Irini, why in heaven did you go to Thessaloniki just before the Council? Why did you not return in time to greet the delegates? You could have headed off this riot!"

Empress Irini drew a deep breath and controlled her

emotions, as I had often seen her do. Still, her voice was low and trembling. "You are right. I should have listened to the bishops. I didn't understand how deep was their fear of being accused of heresy. This won't happen next time."

Constantine's voice rang out in anger. "There will be no next time. I will have the Senate name me Emperor in my own right. The senators are ready and willing. When I lead the Empire, there will be no icons."

He walked out, back straight, head erect, fists clenched. My heart swelled in pride even as I trembled. He knew I had an icon of Saint Thekla. He had seen Brother Grigorios painting icons on the walls of my convent church. When Constantine took the throne, would he destroy our icons and throw us in prison?

Theodore wiped his bruised face with a white silk handkerchief. He broke the stunned silence in a low, quiet voice, unlike his usual rush of words. "Highness, we cannot allow thugs to stop us from bringing holy icons to churches and homes. We cannot fail those faithful who came here expecting to bring their icons out from hiding."

Brother Fanis broke in. "God has given you a mission, Empress Irini. I urge you to hold another God-given council, may you be forever blessed."

Empress Irini's reply was sharp and exasperated. "Of course I will hold another council. Of course I will bring back icons. Did you think I could be cowed by violence?"

I slipped out the door without asking permission and went to Dino's apartment. He was pacing the room and kicking the couch in fury.

"What a disaster! All this meeting has achieved is trouble. If my mother wants to convene another council, I will stop her. She only wants to keep the crown of Empress on her head. But I swear in the name of God that I am going to take it from her and make sure she never gets it back."

This wasn't the first time he had said that his mother intended to keep the crown, nor was it the first time he had said he would stop her. But his rage shocked me. I left the Palace, not wanting to hear a word from either of them. I caught the last ferry to Chalkidon and went straight to the public bathhouse and washed away the sweat and the day. I slept poorly in the stifling dormitory of the Chalkidon convent because my mind kept re-living the awful day. In the morning, I bought bread and cheese and passage on the mail coach to Pendykion. It was crowded with stinking monks and nuns talking excitedly of the fight. Elias was on the coach, looking tired. He gave me a short nod. In Pendykion, I went again to the bathhouse while Elias went to the men's side. We met in his room over the wheelwright. He brought a tin of sliced cucumbers, soft cheeses, and sweet melon. The stifling heat had gone with the sun and a cool breeze was wandering through the window.

"What were you doing there, fighting off that mob?" I demanded. "Who are you working for?"

He finished off the melon, then drew a breath. "Remember when we were walking to Constantinople from Ikonion and we stayed with my Auntie Sofia in Nicaea?"

Of course I remembered Auntie Sofia and her luxurious villa. The attendants in the bathhouse had piled my clean hair on my head and Elias had looked at me with new eyes. I still had the jewelled sandals he gave me although as a nun I could never wear them. "Auntie Sofia said that you and Emperor Leon had grown up together," I remembered.

He nodded. "We were fast friends and he didn't have any others. When he became Emperor, he appointed me postmaster in Pendykion so I could monitor the mail, hear the rumours, and keep him informed of what was going on in the Empire. Just before he died, he was having severe stomach pains. He feared that Irini was poisoning him."

Elias waited for me to say something but I remained silent so he went on. "He also feared for Constantine's safety. He asked me to watch over the boy and see that he was crowned Emperor. I swore under oath that I would."

"Irini would never harm her own son!" I exclaimed.

"He was referring to an attack by his five half-brothers. I begged him to appoint me one of his attendants so I could be near him in case they went after him, but he laughed and said that I would be too bored to do a good job. He said that I was more valuable out in the Empire, watching and listening." His mouth twisted. "I should have insisted. If I had been at Leon's last ceremony, I would have stopped him from putting on that crown."

"How could you possibly have known it would cause the boils that killed him?"

He looked at me straight. "Is Irini planning another council? Tell me so I can protect Constantine from what happened in this one."

I hesitated. Elias had vowed to Emperor Leon to protect Dino, just as I had vowed to Empress Irini to protect her. Were we at cross-purposes? I didn't want Irini and Constantine to come between us. I couldn't imagine my life without Elias. Every week, I watched for his little mail boat and walked down to the village to collect our mail and talk. Just being near him gave me comfort. My nights with him in his little room over the wheelwright gave me strength. On the other hand, although I had known him longer than anyone except my family, I had never met his wealthy Constantinople family or the people he met secretly in his private room in a brothel in Constantinople. All I knew was that he used to work for the Office of the Eparch of the Monasteries visiting monasteries to see if abbots were abusing the monks. It sounded far-fetched. Still, my heart trusted him.

"Yes, Irini wants another council," I replied. "Constantine is dead set against it. He said that he would make the Senate name him Emperor, and that when he leads the Empire, there would be no icons. He insists that Irini only wants a council so that she can gain power to become Empress in her own right."

"Of course she wants to be Empress in her own right. Leon told me that the day he was wed," he snapped.

A month later, Constantine came out to Prinkypos. He was in a dark mood. I sat with him under a tree in the plateia and watched him rip a pine cone to shreds.

"My mother has set the date for another council: September twenty-fourth, a year from now. The papal bishops are staying in Constantinople for it."

"Won't the army and the Palace Guard break it up, as they did before?"

His face grew darker. "The bishops were the real organizers. They gave the signal to start the riot. Stavrakios and Aetios are ferreting out their names. My mother says she will have the leaders defrocked, flogged, and exiled. The followers will lose their bishoprics."

"Will the next council be in Holy Apostles Church again?"

"No, in Nicaea. The Church of the Dormition. That's where the very first Ecumenical Council was held, when they wrote the Nicene Creed centuries ago. This will make the bishops happy. The monks like Nicaea because it is near the monasteries in Bithynia where they are still painting icons."

I remembered my own journey through Nicaea and nodded. "Delegates from the eastern Empire can come by main road, and delegates from the west can take a boat to Gebze and walk a half day. There are plenty of inns and monasteries in Nicaea. But won't there be the same trouble?"

He threw up his hands. "My mother has a plan, which she won't tell me. Patriarch Tarasios and Theodore and Brother Fanis know but not me—and I am Emperor! I am fifteen and she has not let me see battle. My uncles Anthimos and Evdokimos are near my age and they have seen battle. Harun al-Rashid is only five years older and he is commanding entire armies! I have had military training since I was ten. I am good with the sword and the lance and I am an excellent horseman! But my mother won't let me speak to the commanding generals about their campaigns, and she cuts me off when I try to say anything to my advisors in the Consistory. I am an emperor without a voice."

I had never seen him so angry. It was the deep, bitter rage of an emperor denied his rightful place on the throne.

That winter, Commander Tatzates, who had defected to the Caliph four years before, died fighting the Khazars. That same year, Caliph al-Mahdi died and Empress Irini gained the most powerful enemy of her life, the new Caliph, Harun al-Rashid.

Chapter IX

Constantine came to Prinkypos in early Lent and stayed until Holy Week, as he had done the previous Lent, and for the same reason: Irini was blocking him from joining the planning meetings for her council. He ranted about it from the moment he arrived.

"Theodore and his uncle, Abbott Platon, are writing the speeches for Patriarch Tarasios. Brother Fanis is helping them—and no one will show me what they are writing. I don't even know what is on the agenda. All she will tell me is that it is being called the Seventh Ecumenical Council to show that it is a legitimate council, following the other six. Why do we need to officially bring back icons?" he exploded. "People have lived without icons for over sixty years. My mother is scorning the army and the priests—and only to make herself popular with the monks and the people so they will back her when she tries to be Empress in her own right. Well, I won't let her."

His mouth twisted in anger. "Now my mother tells

me that I must sign a Declaration of Faith at the end, stating that I believe every paragraph that the delegates have agreed on by vote! I won't do it, Auntie Thekla! In two years, when I am Emperor in my own right, I will declare everything she did to be null and void!"

He went back to Constantinople and didn't return, only because Irini let him train with his military unit at the army base in Evdomon, five miles from Constantinople. She did it just to keep him away from the Palace, he wrote me. But in July, the baking heat and stench of pisspots and animal dung in Constantinople drove them both to the island. Constantine and his guards stayed in their cottages in the village and Irini took over my study, complaining about Constantine.

"The child battles me about the council every moment of every day," she exploded, throwing herself into the big chair under the shady grape arbour. "He insists there will be another fight. He's wrong."

"How can you be so sure, Highness?" I asked, tossing scraps to the chickens.

"Because I will not be there to provoke those misogynists. Patriarch Tarasios will direct the proceedings, beginning to end. Those fool bishops will believe that he is the organizer."

"Constantine says you won't allow him in the planning meetings."

"And I won't allow him into the Council in Nicaea, either. He will start shouting that it is not legal because he as Emperor has not convened it. Well, he's not Emperor in his own right yet, so he can't convene anything. Stavrakios won't be there either, nor Aetios or any of my eunuchs except for Nikitas. He will attend the final session to make sure Patriarch Tarasios wraps it up properly."

She turned her intense gaze on me. "You, however, will go. You will attend all the sessions. You will be my eyes and ears. After every session, you will write a report for me and send it by courier to Pendykion. Stavrakios will be staying there. I will be on Prinkypos and Stavrakios will bring over your reports. Prinkypos is a day closer to Nicaea than Constantinople and I can keep a finger on the proceedings."

My heart sank. I had no wish to see monks and priests punching each other. Even if they didn't fight, I would have to sit through long days of stinking, shouting men. "Aren't you worried that there will be trouble?"

Her smile dripped with satisfaction. "The bishops who caused the riot are in prison, in exile, or they are barred from the proceedings. I am allowing only bishops who declare under oath that they will accept my agenda."

"The Palace Guard and the army could break it up."

"Stavrakios and Aetios and I have a plan. A few days before the Council begins, I will order the Palace Guard to rush to Malagina, to the imperial horse breeding farm. I will say that I have received word that the Caliph's armies are on their way to steal the horses, as they are wont to do. The Palace Guard are always first to defend Malagina because they are closer than the theme armies."

My thoughts wandered to the lush Malagina Valley where Elias and I had seen the magnificent warhorses and colts on our way to Constantinople. We had made love in a hayloft and I had wished our journey would never end.

"When the Palace Guard are out of the city," Irini went on, pulling my thoughts back to the present, "I will bring in the army of Thrace and appoint them as my new Palace Guard. I will call them the Vigla. Thrace is far to the northwest and the army is less involved with the politics of Constantinople than the other theme armies. Also, they know me personally. Constantine and I have travelled through Thrace twice in the last two years. Stavrakios has already gone to give them orders." Irini's smile reeked of secrecy. I could understand Constantine's fury.

That afternoon, I went down to the village and walked with Constantine by the sea. "Your mother says there won't be any trouble in Nicaea. She and Stavrakios and Aetios have a plan."

"Don't believe her. Those two eunuchs lie to her and her advisors are too afraid of her to tell her the truth. My eunuchs have found out that Patriarch Tarasios is sending invitations only to the bishops who won't cause trouble."

"How does she know who they are?"

"They will be the bishops who can prove that they have remained faithful to icons. Those who cannot prove this will be admitted only if they agree to stand before everyone at the council and confess that they have conspired to disrupt the previous council, or have persecuted people who venerated icons. They must say that they regret their actions and recant their beliefs. It's cruel revenge, is all it is, Auntie Thekla, and it will happen during the first session to make sure that everyone sees their humiliation and is afraid to cause trouble. My mother has compiled a long list of clergy to humiliate. The bishop from the Church of Blachernae is top of the list."

"Why do these bishops want to attend, if they know they will face humiliation and scorn?"

"Because she and Tarasios have taken away their bishoprics. If they grovel, they might get them back. Otherwise, they will be wandering the roads begging for food. No monastery will let them in, that's certain."

That evening, Empress Irini made me read aloud the recanting speech that she, Patriarch Tarasios, Theodore, and Brother Fanis had drafted. She wanted to hear how it sounded to the ear. For the first time in my life, I felt sorry for a bishop. These men had obeyed the ban on icons their entire lives and now they were to be publicly humiliated and punished for it. Worse, what they were confessing to would soon be deemed heresy! My heart felt a twinge of pity. Then I remembered their thick winter boots and heavy cloaks, and how their well-fed bodies had shoved me aside in the narrow lanes of Constantinople. In fact, as I read the recanting paragraphs aloud, I started looking forward to observing the Council at work.

"There will be seven sessions," Irini explained, "each devoted to one issue. The most important issue is that devotion to painted images is acceptable and necessary. I have ordered Patriarch Tarasios to finish each session quickly. I don't want long discussions to lead the vote astray."

So, in late September, one year after I had watched the Ecumenical Council at Holy Apostles church break up into fist fights and clashing swords, I was crowded in a coach with Elias and some rank-smelling monks bumping along the coastal road to Nicaea. Sixteen years before, I had walked this road with Elias going to Constantinople, pretending that I was a nun and that Elias was my monk cousin. How strange the passage of time! I had known nothing of Irini or Constantinople and my future had been as hazy as a summer's day. Now I was Abbess Thekla, Irini was Empress, and I knew Constantinople like the back of my hand. But I was still lying that I was a nun.

I gazed at Elias with fond curiosity, wondering if he too were remembering that journey. He was as tall and muscular as ever and still had his charming smile, but threads of silver brightened his thick dark hair. He had told me that he was going to Nicaea because the postal way-station there needed extra help during the council. It sounded suspicious. He was probably spying for someone. But who?

Priests and monks were clogging the road in such numbers that we made slow progress. At the port of Gebze, so many clerics were climbing off boats that our guards had to ride ahead of the carriage and let their horses clear a path. It was dusk when we climbed out stiffly at the Nicaea postal way-station and elbowed through the packs of clerics taking over the streets. The stench of public toilets, garbage swill in the gutters, and charcoal smoke was choking. What a relief to stagger through the gates of Auntie Sofia's villa and collapse under her fragrant jasmine vine. Elias had written to her explaining my mission, and she had quickly written back with an offer of hospitality. Unfortunately, Empress Irini had arranged a room for me in a convent because she wanted me to hear the nuns' gossip about the Council.

Auntie Sofia greeted me with near awe. In the torchlight, her hair was still henna-red and chains of pearls clanked around her plump throat. Tears caked the powder on her cheeks when I gave her the small icon that Brother Grigorios had made for her. She would have kissed my hand if I hadn't yanked it away. Her housekeeper showed me to the same lovely guest room. I approached the polished silver mirror with caution and held up my candle to my reflection. With relief, I saw a face that had changed little and no silver threads in my chestnut hair. The housekeeper took me to Auntie Sofia's private bath and after that I was dining on food so delicious that I wished I weren't too tired to enjoy it.

I stayed only two luxurious nights, hearing her gossip and dodging her questions about the Palace. Then I moved into the small Convent of Saint Ermina. I was grateful that Empress Irini had given me such a fat purse for the Abbess because I got a quiet, cool cell that opened to a garden shaded by a kitron tree. I needed peace and privacy to write my daily reports. Each evening, I would take them to the postal way-station. By the next morning, Empress Irini would know what had been accomplished. Patriarch Tarasios was likely sending her his own version.

The next morning, I went to the Church of the Dormition and presented my letter of introduction from

Empress Irini to a slovenly monk lounging behind a long table in the vestibule. He and other monks were checking off names on long parchments.

"Balcony," he muttered and jerked his shaved head towards some narrow stairs.

The balcony was solid with restless, muttering monks but some nuns were occupying a corner and I squeezed in with them. Below, I could see Elias wandering around in his imperial post tunica, collecting letters the delegates wanted to send. Theodore was chatting with Brother Fanis. Finally, Patriarch Tarasios opened the proceedings with a long prayer. Hours later, I staggered out, suffocated by the rank air and numbed by the endless blare of male voices. Living in a community of women, one forgets how loud men's voices are and how they never cease interrupting each other. And how they stink.

Elias was waiting outside. He smelled as bad as the monks now crowding the eateries. I kept my scarf over my mouth and nose. "I want to write my report now before I forget everything," I gasped, stumbling in the direction of Saint Ermina convent.

He steered me the other way and stopped at a food stall not crowded with monks. "Eat something; it will help you remember."

He was right. The sweet buns flavoured with mastic and filled with date paste and ground walnuts cleared my head, as did the sweetened kitron juice. Elias walked me to the convent and said he would wait outside and take me to the postal way-station.

I settled at my small desk, laid out the quills, ink, and papyrus I had brought from Prinkypos, and turned my thoughts to the past day.

"Greetings Esteemed Empress Irini, 24 September, Session One. Today the delegates signed in. This took hours because the clerks had to locate each name on parchments and make a mark. Every session will begin this way. A scribe told me there were 257 names. The bishops from Antioch, Jerusalem, and Alexandria couldn't get here. They are represented by two monks whose names I don't know. I sat in the balcony with some nuns and a lot of stinking monks who were not accepted to the Council but could listen. When Patriarch Tarasios started speaking, they shouted that he was not qualified to convene the Council because he had been appointed by Empress Irini. He paid no attention and began accusing certain bishops of causing the uproar at last year's Council. I couldn't hear well because of the shouting monks. I did hear the confessions of the bishops since everyone went quiet for that. They wept and apologized over and over for their acts against the previous Council and against icons. The delegates will vote later whether to give them back their bishoprics. Session two is the day after tomorrow. Everyone already needs a rest. Faithful in Your Service, Thekla, Abbess of the Convent of the Theotokos on Prinkypos."

Elias now stank of strong wine. I looked at him sternly. "I trust you are not too drunk to get us to the postal way-station."

"Drinking with these clerics is the only way to learn what is happening in the back rooms," he slurred.

"Why do you need to know? Who are you reporting to?" I demanded.

He pretended not to hear. "Auntie Sofia wants you to dine with us this evening. She is eager to hear about the session."

I quickly refused, alarmed at what Elias might blurt out in his drunken state about how we had slept together on our journey to Constantinople, and how we continued to meet in his bed in Pendykion. "I am dining at the head table with the Abbess," I lied.

Elias drunkenly grabbed my sleeve. "Please come," he begged. Tears shone in his brown eyes. "I hardly ever see you when you are on Prinkypos. Now I can see you every day."

I pried off his fingers, pleased, although I suspected that this was the wine speaking. "Tomorrow I will accept. Try to stay sober."

I had brought from my room a clean tunica, scarf, and underclothes, so after we went to the postal way-station, I continued to the bathhouse. I could not sleep in the convent's clean linen sheets with the stink of monks clinging to me. The bath was refreshing although the price had risen shockingly since I was there last. I gave the attendant my clothes to wash—another exorbitant sum from my purse.

The next day I wandered around Nicaea with some nuns from Nikomidia. The goods in the shop windows were far inferior to Constantinople. Many icons were for sale. They were poorly made, clearly slapped together in haste for the ready market of monks and nuns who were snapping them up. But how wonderful to see icons freely displayed, no matter the quality! Women were showing them to children and telling them that now they could talk to a saint. I caught sight of Elias, drinking with some monks.

He had sobered up by evening when we dined with Auntie Sofia, but he spoke little. His eyes were blood-shot and his fingers trembled. His hair was damp and he reeked of the cheap jasmine scent they pour on you in the bathhouse. He was wearing what looked like a new tunica.

Auntie Sofia's servants served us a lavish supper and she pumped me for details about the session. The excel-lent red wine loosened my tongue so, while I devoured cuttlefish cooked in their ink, grilled barbunia straight from the sea, and fried pumpkin drizzled with honey and sprinkled with raisins and walnuts, I related the events and my opinion of the participants which was not good. I confess I took pleasure in having Auntie Sofia's gaze so fixed upon me that her chubby hand often paused half-way to her mouth. The final course was sweet pears and quince steeped in wine and nutmeg. I almost regret-ted having to decline her frenzied invitation to stay the night, but I liked the privacy of my quiet convent room. The wool-stuffed mattress was comfortable although the previous evening's meal and breakfast had been inedi-ble. Elias walked me there, saying I needed protection from the drunken monks, as if he hadn't witnessed many times my skill with the knife on my belt. I felt an odd frustration being so near him. If we were in Pendykion, I would be in his bed. I wondered if he felt the same.

"I miss you," he slurred, reaching for my arm and answering my unspoken thought.

"I miss you too." I dodged his hand because we had

reached the convent and the nun at the door was watching us.

The convent breakfast was sour millet porridge, by the foul odour coming from the kitchen, so I went out to the street and found a food stall serving boiled cracked-wheat porridge made with goat milk. The vendor filled my wooden bowl and I paid extra for an egg and chopped almonds. I needed nourishment for the long day. I registered, found a seat in the balcony, and spread out the shawl I had brought to sit on. I sprinkled some jasmine perfume that I had purchased the previous day on my scarf before I wrapped it over my mouth and nose. Still, by the end of the day, I was dizzy from the fetid air. Elias was waiting outside.

"You look like you are going to faint," he said and led me to a kapelarion near the city gates that boasted fresh air and equally fresh oysters.

I wolfed down twelve of them and downed a pile of warm flatbread smeared with fish paste. It gave me energy to write my second letter.

"Greetings Esteemed Augusta Irini, 26 September, Session Two. The delegates signed in more quickly today, clearly eager to watch Patriarch Tarasios go after more weeping bishops and hear their tearful confessions. He started with the bishop of Neokaisaria who was a very old man with a long white beard and stooped shoulders that shook when he sobbed out that he had been at the Council of Hieria convened by Emperor Constantine. He confessed through his tears that he had voted to ban icons. He pleaded for forgiveness and wept he would confess to any errors, whatever they were. It was pathetic. I was embarrassed for him. I would never make my nuns suffer such a degrading experience.

"Patriarch Tarasios told him to write a statement for the next session and the delegates would vote as to whether he could resume his bishopric. After that, there were so many bishops pushing forward with tearful confessions that I grew bored. Finally, Patriarch Tarasios put an end to their weeping by reading a letter from Pope Adrianos, describing the veneration of icons as he practiced it. I didn't see much difference from ours but I couldn't hear well because of the monks shouting that they didn't care about any heretic pope. They used language which you don't want to know. Session number three will be in two days' time. Faithful in your service, Thekla, Abbess, Convent of the Theotokos on Prinkypos."

I woke up Elias, who was sleeping against the convent wall, and handed him my letter to take to the courier. I went to the bathhouse with my clean clothes. I had never bathed so much but I couldn't sleep with the stench of men's sweat on me. I did not sleep well, partly because of the bellowing of drunken monks and partly because the thin watery lentil soup that the convent had served for supper left me with bowel problems and a hungry stomach. I missed Aspasia's cooking. I missed the fresh air and exercise on Prinkypos. In the morning, I went out to hunt for breakfast. Elias was outside, leaning against the wall looking ill.

"Find me something decent to eat," I demanded. "The Abbess should be ashamed of her kitchen. I shall report her to the Eparch of the Monasteries."

Elias knew a good pastry stall so we filled our stomachs

and my satchel with pastries stuffed with figs, cherries, and cooked apple. The vendor poured sour cherry juice in my tin cup, sour enough to make my tongue tingle, and added some sort of fragrant flower. We strolled out the city gates and along Lake Askania, dodging beggars and salesmen hawking glass vials containing air from the Holy Land and water from the Jordan River. I almost bought an olive wood cross from the Mount of Olives until the lying salesman told me that all his crosses were embedded with thorns from the Crown of Thorns.

"And now the crown has no thorns?" I scolded the salesman, who laughed.

"What is your opinion of the council so far?" Elias asked.

I thought that over. "These meetings are about who holds the power and how they are crushing the others. If Empress Irini wanted only to bring back icons, Patriarch Tarasios could have delivered that the first morning."

We had a lovely day. We walked to a tiny village on the lake that boasted an excellent kapelarion. I devoured steamed mussels, fava beans topped with chopped onions, fried cheese on crunchy bread, and mushrooms fried in garlic oil.

"We're on the road to Saint Emmelia convent," Elias said, pointing at the mountains in the near distance. "After all this is over, why don't we go there? Autumn is a perfect time to walk in the mountains. Sixteen years ago, we slept together under the stars."

Tears came to my eyes as I remembered our days and nights in those lovely mountains. I was so tempted, I almost said yes. Then I came to my senses. "Empress

Irini will be waiting for me on Prinkypos," I said, with regret. But I kept thinking about Elias during the next session, which was so boring that I got a headache.

"Greetings Empress Irini. 28 September, Session Three. The Council approved re-admitting Grigorios of Neokaisaria into the Council, along with several others. Three bishops recanted their opposition to the veneration of icons. They were pardoned and allowed to keep their bishoprics and also take part in the Council. Seven more bishops quickly recanted and demanded that they also be admitted as delegates. They were pardoned but not allowed straightway to resume their bishoprics. Patriarch Tarasios read a letter which he had sent to the three Eastern Patriarchs in Antioch, Jerusalem and Alexandria containing his Confession of Faith. The delegates approved the letter. Patriarch Tarasios ended the day by proclaiming the end of strife, saying that East, West, North and South were now united. Anyone who believes that after watching these three sessions will believe anything. Faithful in Your Service, Abbess, Convent of the Theotokos on Prinkypos."

Elias was sleeping against the convent wall. I woke him up and we walked to the postal way-station where I handed my report to the courier and Elias and I went on to a kapelarion. We ordered a shoulder of lamb between us and cheese-stuffed aubergine. It didn't cure my headache but it was nice sitting across from Elias and looking at his handsome, although pale, face.

"Like old times in Constantinople," I said, rubbing my head. He took my hands, astonishing me. Men did not touch women in public.

"I need to tell you something. It's about me. Who I really am."

My headache vanished. I waited, my eyes on his wine-flushed face and trim beard. "Once, I told you that I was an investigator for the Eparch of the Monasteries."

"You said that you stayed in monasteries to see whether the abbots were abusing the monks."

"Did you believe me?"

"Not really. Was it a lie?"

"Not entirely. I was also spying for Emperor Constantine, young Constantine's grandfather."

I frowned. "I thought he was your enemy. I thought he had executed your uncle for conspiracy to seize the throne."

"True. But Leon, his son and my dear friend, persuaded him to let me investigate the charges of conspiracy. I discovered that the charges had been invented whole cloth by several bishops who hated my uncle for reversing his belief in icons and leading the Council of Hieria to ban them. I reported this to Emperor Constantine. He listened carefully and had my uncle beheaded anyway." He stabbed the lamb shoulder viciously with his knife.

I remembered what Irini had said years before. "Emperor Constantine told Irini that he didn't care whether your uncle was innocent or guilty, that the Church was gaining too much power and a popular patriarch had to go."

He drained his wine cup and waved it at the kapelarios for more. "The bishops I had investigated then told Emperor Constantine that I was part of the conspiracy. I was forced to flee to Antioch in the Caliphate."

"And now you are watching over Constantine. You told me."

"Which is why you must tell me what Irini is up to."

I put down my knife. "I vowed loyalty to her. I vowed to protect her. I will not spy on her for you. I cannot harm her."

"She wants to be Empress in her own right, Constantine believes. How is she going to get past him? He is the acknowledged Emperor."

His words struck my heart cold. "How can you be protecting Constantine if you are in Pendykion?" I fumbled. "You must be working with someone inside the Palace."

He looked at me straight. "Yes. Others in the Great Palace are watching over him. People who were loyal to Emperor Constantine and to Leon. We communicate."

"Who?" I demanded.

But then a courier hurried up and murmured in his ear and he left in a hurry. I finished my meal, ignoring the stares of the people around me at a woman eating alone. My thoughts swirled like the wine in my cup. I kept thinking about Constantine, the child I never had, the child who held my heart. Whom was I loyal to first, Constantine or Irini? I was still thinking when I walked back to the convent.

The following day, I took a pen and sheets of papyrus with me to the session to make notes and help me remember. I had to ask the nun next to me to hold my bottle of ink and she did so on the condition that I write a letter to her sister. The other nuns demanded the same. I didn't mind as it made the time pass quickly. Thanks to my notes, I also wrote my report more quickly.

"Esteemed Empress Augusta, Session Four. A scribe told me that three hundred and thirty-five delegates signed in today. Your Grace told me that you gave Patriarch Tarasios instructions to close each session quickly. Today, he let the debates drag on and on. He said, and I wrote this down, 'We are here to heal the rifts within the imperial church with the minimum of disruption and internal wrangling.' I suppose he was telling those monks who had lost their ears and tongues for being faithful to icons that they should be satisfied with their persecutors getting off with a slap on the wrist. The monks sitting around me didn't like it and I agree with them. Faithful in your service, Abbess Thekla of the Convent of the Theotokos on Prinkypos."

My single letter about Sessions Four and Five was short.

"1 and 4 October, All Faithful Empress Augusta. Please forgive my letter today that concerns two sessions. I couldn't understand the theology that the Council voted on. Patriarch Tarasios spoke for hours. What lungs that man has. He proved that icons were holy and should be venerated by reading a lot of scripture which I don't remember. He said that Moses painted images of the cherubim on God's orders. Our village priest never mentioned this. Patriarch Tarasios also said that all the angels that had ever been seen were pictured as people. Does that mean that angels walk among us and we are unknowing of their presence? I will ask Father Dimitrios. Patriarch Tarasios explained the difference between worshipping an image and the veneration of an image.

Here it is: Veneration is not paying homage to the image but to the saint. Faithful in Your Service, Abbess Thekla."

The next day was a rest day. In a shop, I purchased some decent icons of women saints for my nuns and novices. There was not a large selection, for which I gave a stern lecture to the slovenly iconographer. I was thoroughly sick of the stinking streets of Nicaea and hoped that Auntie Sofia would invite me to supper but Elias said he wanted to eat alone with me this last time. I thought he would tell me whom he was spying for but he would not answer my questions. I went to bed dreading the next day's shouting clergy and my struggles to remember what they had said.

"Esteemed Empress, Seventh and last session, thank God. Three hundred and six tired delegates signed in today, still arguing. The Council passed a decree that images of Christ, Mother of God, angels, and saints are to be painted on wood, vessels, garments and walls for salutation and honour. There is no difference between a painting and a statue, or how the saint is painted. Images are to stand next to candles and incense. All Christians are to adore them. Every church must have a relic of a saint. Whoever refuses to obey is a heretic. Faithful in your service, Thekla, Abbess, Convent of the Theotokos on Prinkypos."

After handing my letter to a very drunken and smelly Elias, I went to the bathhouse for my final scrub. When I came out, Elias was waiting outside, having had a scrub himself. We consumed an unremarkable meal at a kapelarion but spoke little. Both of us were dropping with fatigue.

I climbed into my convent bed for the last time and savoured the peaceful room, mindful that the next day I would be hard at work picking grapes and olives on Prinkypos. The next morning, Elias and I consumed boiled cracked-wheat porridge sprinkled with almonds and kitron flower water. We walked in silence to the postal way-station. Grouchy hungover monks and priests climbed into our carriage, forcing me to cover my mouth and nose with my jasmine-scented scarf. As the coach clattered out the gates, I looked at Lake Askania sparkling in the October sun and thought what a relief it was to be leaving the stinking, stifling, narrow streets of Nicaea and the gutters running with the piss of delegates. What a relief to be away from the Church of the Dormition and the stink of unwashed monks.

"If I never hear another speech, it will be too soon," I said to Elias over the snores of the clerics.

"One more meeting is set for October twenty-third in Magnavra Palace," he said. "Patriarch Tarasios will describe what happened in Nicaea and read out the Declaration of Faith that the Council has approved by vote. Emperor Constantine and the delegates will acclaim it with their signatures."

It was a full week before the stink of the Church of the Dormition left my nostrils and I could think clearly. Hundreds of delegates had voted to reverse the edicts of the previous ecumenical council as well as the edicts of two emperors. Did that mean that icons were with us forever? Or would Constantine, angry at his mother, convene another council and make the bishops vote to ban them again? I found out when Constantine came

148

out to Prinkypos a few weeks later. We sat with our feet in the warm sea but his anger chilled my heart.

"I'm not signing the Declaration of Faith," he fumed. "Why should I? I was denied any of the planning. I was barred from attending. I'm not signing something that other people cooked up!"

"Have you read the proceedings?"

"I have indeed and I don't like it. Making those bishops recant in front of hundreds of other bishops and monks—such unnecessary humiliation! These bishops had obeyed the law and they were shamed for it! My mother and her hand-picked Patriarch have denied the beliefs of three generations of Isaurian emperors! If I sign that Declaration, I dishonour their memories. I will not allow a cleric to tell me how to rule my Empire. I understand why my grandfather executed his first Patriarch."

"Have you told your mother that you aren't signing the Declaration of Faith? It won't become an edict without your signature."

He set his jaw stubbornly. "My mother has advanced the date for the final session. It will be the third week in November. I'll send the yacht for you. You can see what I will do."

That night, I lay in bed, thinking. Was Constantine being loyal to the Isaurian emperors before him? Or was he simply angry that his mother had excluded him in every part of the process and this was his revenge?

He signed. My poor sweet Dino sat on a dais beside his mother and signed in the presence of representatives of the army, Palace Guard, officers of state, scarlet-robed priests, dull-robed monks, and delegates—watched by the wealthy and connected of Constantinople who pushed their lavishly-dressed bodies into the vast, gold-plated Magnavra Palace. Patriarch Tarasios stood at one side of the dais in his brilliant red patriarchal robes and read out the Declaration of Faith and the acclamations and anathemas that the delegates had voted in during those long days at the Church of the Dormition. He handed the document to Stavrakios as Patrikios and Minister of the Post and Transportation. Stavrakios carried it across the dais and placed it on a table in front of Constantine. Reluctantly and sullenly, Constantine signed his name on the Declaration of Faith and brought icons back into churches and homes, even though he didn't want to.

The delegates who had managed to get to Constantinople passed by the table and signed. Brother Fanis signed as Abbott of the Abbey of the Great Acre. I know because I read it over later in Empress Irini's chambers.

After all the scribbling was over, Stavrakios carried the Declaration of Faith back to Patriarch Tarasios and bowed it into his hands. Patriarch Tarasios bowed to Empress Irini and Emperor Constantine who gave him restrained nods. It was over.

Later, Constantine and I stood by the window in Empress Irini's reception room and watched her celebrate with Patriarch Tarasios, Theodore, and Abbott Fanis—her collaborators who had drafted everything that the delegates had signed. Irini was jubilant. Exhausted, nerves still on edge, but exultant.

Her brilliant smile slipped only when Theodore announced with solemn piety that he and his father and brothers were taking the vows of poverty and entering the monastery of his uncle, Abbott Platon, in Bithynia. Theodore's mother would take the vows at a nearby convent. They had sold their worldly goods and transferred their property to the poor.

Again, the veils of time parted for me and I saw into the future. Theodore was beginning his rise to power.

Chapter X

Constantine's fury over the Council of Nicaea cast a melancholy shadow for me over the Nativity celebrations which normally gave me so much pleasure. I felt no joy watching Father Dimitrios bless the fishing boats on Nativity morning or hearing him chant the beautiful liturgies. Aspasia decided I wasn't eating enough and she kept bringing food to my study and watching me eat. Sister Efthia brewed up vile herbal concoctions which she forced me to choke down. Sister Matrona told me to pull myself together.

"Melancholy is self-indulgence masked as worry," she snapped. "Do not inflict it on the rest of us."

I made an effort to cheer up but it wasn't until early Lent when the island glimmered with red poppies that my mood lifted. Megalo's excited call hurried us to look over the wall. The imperial yacht was passing below the convent and my beloved Constantine was waving madly from the deck.

Constantine came bounding up the lane and we sat

on the bench by the cemetery. Rather, I sat while he paced, angry words pouring from him like dried lentils from a jar. His guards lounged farther down the lane, enjoying the February sun.

"My mother has summoned the Frankish ambassador to Magnavra Palace and cancelled my engagement to Rotrud!" he shouted. "Nothing I say can change her mind. Come back to the Palace with me now, Auntie Thekla. Make her call back the ambassador. There's still time."

"I thought you didn't want to marry this girl," I said, astonished but also relieved. Now my beloved Dino wouldn't be living on the other side of the world.

"I didn't want to marry her, at first. Then I realised that when I am at the court of the Franks, I will be out of my mother's control. But now she has cancelled my freedom!"

"Why?" I puzzled. "She started plotting your betrothal to that girl when you were nine. King Charles signed the agreement five years ago and the Pope finally put his blessing on it."

He threw himself on the grass beside my bench. "Here's why: a message has come from the two eunuchs my mother sent to Charles's court to tutor Rotrud in Greek. They write that Charles will hand over his throne only to a son of his blood. Never to me."

"After all these years, they just learned this?" I exclaimed.

"They didn't speak the language for a long time. And they are fools! I am even more angry that I had to get this news from my eunuchs—and they got it from my mother's eunuchs. Those tutors should have sent the message to me! I'm Emperor! Now my mother says that she has summoned the tutors home. She tells me nothing! She is treating me like a child."

He snatched up a stone and flung it furiously at a tree. "Ever since I was eleven, I have believed I would be King of the Franks. I have learned Latin and German and some French. I told my mother that I will go to Aachen and speak to Charles myself. I can speak his language after all these years of study. But my mother said she will have me locked in my chambers if I try to leave the Empire. She can't do this to me! I'm the Emperor!"

"She can," I said sadly. "She is Regent."

His eyes narrowed. "I am seventeen. My advisors tell me that the Senate and I together could pass an edict that forces my mother to step down now. They are willing. But my mother and Stavrakios and Aetios control the Palace guards and eunuchs. The Senate and I could pass this edict but we don't have the force to make her step down. I have to wait until January when the Senate will crown me Emperor in my own right."

He flung another rock at a tree. "Our Empire needs good relations with Charles of the Franks. That was the whole point of my betrothal. I would be content to sit on the throne of the Romans of the East with Rotrud beside me as my empress. But my mother says she will find me another bride."

A foreboding came over me. "Does she have someone in mind?"

"A bride show! A stupid parade of ugly females hiding their big noses under veils!"

I tried not to laugh. "So choose the least ugly. You only have to visit her bed once a year."

His voice grew desperate. "She won't allow even that! She and Stavrakios will choose my bride, she says."

I spoke gently. "All parents choose the brides for their sons. Especially emperors. Your great-grandfather chose your grandfather's bride. Your grandfather chose your father's bride."

"And look what he got." He glanced at the guards and lowered his voice. "Stavrakios is behind this bride show. He wants the throne but a eunuch cannot be emperor. So he will marry one of his female relatives to me, and she will poison me and her brother will seize the throne."

I started to laugh, then sobered. The horrible truth was that Stavrakios could do that.

"Talk to my mother, Auntie Thekla. Tell her to give up this bride show. Come January, I will be Emperor in my own right. I will choose my own bride and my mother can do nothing about it."

Resigned to a futile mission, I put Sister Matrona in charge and got on the yacht.

Empress Irini grew more beautiful every year. She was thirty-six that year and looked half that. She ate like a mule and never got plump. Her thick chestnut hair glowed and her skin shone with herbal creams blended by the Palace apothecaries. Her hands were smooth and the nails firm. I, too, was thirty-six that year. I was slim because I worked off every bite, but my hands and arms were sun-brown and my nails stained by soil.

Irini didn't seem surprised to see me. She waved us to a couch and Nikitas brought over a tray of warm flatbread spread with soft goat cheese and covered with sliced radishes. Irini waited until we had eaten it all before she spoke.

"Constantine wants to marry Rotrud and he has brought you here to persuade me not to cancel his betrothal," she said.

"Yes, Highness," I mumbled through a full mouth.

Constantine drank off a glass of cold wine. "Mother, we need an alliance with King Charles and my marriage will achieve that. I don't care that I will never sit on the Frankish throne. It is only right that Charles passes it to a son of his blood. I will live here as Emperor with Rotrud as my empress."

Irini shook her head. "Aetios is suspicious of Charles. He warned me that Charles wants to take over the entire Christian world. He will come with his army for the wedding and his soldiers will take over the Palace and then the Empire. We will become a puppet state. Charles invaded Lombardia to attach it to his Frankish kingdom."

As much as I loathed Aetios, I had to admit that he had a point.

Irini's voice hardened. "Our ambassadors to the court of King Charles have informed me that Charles has said recently, more than once, and publicly, that a woman cannot rule an empire. Charles is referring to me."

Constantine frowned. "Mother, in January, I will be Emperor in my own right. You will not be Regent."

Empress Irini shouted so suddenly that Nikitas dropped a bowl of fish paste. "I will still be Empress! I will not be put aside! Not by Charles of the Franks and not by you!"

I froze. Constantine didn't move, only stared straight at her. Irini drew a breath and calmed her voice. "Dino, my sweet, give up your dreams of Rotrud. I have thirteen suitable candidates coming to the bride show. I will choose the best one for you."

Constantine's voice was equally calm. "Mother, I will choose my own wife, just as my grandfather Constantine chose his second wife and his third."

"Don't be silly, dear," she snapped, losing her temper again. "Your grandfather was Emperor when his first wife died. Of course he chose his second and third wives."

"I will be Emperor in January. When I am crowned, I will choose Rotrud."

I spoke, hoping to head off more shouting. "Do you favour a certain bride, Highness?"

She gave Constantine a parting glare. "Maria of Amnia, although I have yet to meet her. She comes from a moneyed family in Paphlagonia on the Pontus Sea. Her grandfather was called Filaretos the Merciful because he gave so much to the poor. Maria is said to be pleasant in appearance and demeanour. And she is literate."

Constantine choked back his reply and changed the subject. "While we are discussing what you are doing behind my back, tell me if what I hear about Adalgisos is true. Are you really giving that imbecile an army to take back Lombardia?"

"Adalgisos?" I inquired.

Constantine turned to me. "Adalgisos is the son of the former king of Lombardia. Fifteen years ago, King Charles invaded Lombardia and Adalgisos fled to our gates, begging for sanctuary. My grandfather granted it.

Since then, every year without fail, Adalgisos has come to my mother, begging for an army to take back Lombardia. Now I hear that my mother has agreed to this absurd request."

Irini nodded with a smile. "Adalgisos brought me a letter signed by Duke Arechis of Benevento. He proposes that he and two other dukes join their armies to ours and take back Lombardia. Adalgisos will be king."

Constantine exploded. "You believe this letter? Adalgisos probably wrote it himself."

"He lacks the wits. And the letter had all the proper seals. We could finally rid ourselves of this boring Adalgisos and show Charles that we are a force to be reckoned with. I am sending an army unit with Adalgisos to Sicily. They will join our army in Sicily and march to Lombardia where the dukes will be waiting. Jointly, they will drive the army of King Charles from Lombardia." Irini held up her hand to Constantine's protest. "I gave him this army on the condition that Lombardia becomes our buffer state. Charles will not be able to march blithely into Calabria and Sicily whenever he feels like it."

Constantine stared at his mother in disbelief. "You can't be serious, Mother. King Charles will go to Lombardia himself for the pleasure of slaughtering us. Then he will continue onward and take Sicily and Calabria. You are waving a red flag in front of a bull!"

She held up her hand. "I have appointed Ioannis as commander. I named him commander of the combined armies of Asia. Now he can prove himself."

Constantine forced his voice to stay calm. "Mother, Ioannis is a eunuch you promoted out of your household. Charles will mow him down like he mowed down the Lombard army. Besides, our Treasury doesn't have the funds to transport an army all that distance."

"Of course they have the money. We haven't launched a major campaign in two years. I have ordered the Finance Ministry to stop paying tribute to the Thief of Baghdad. What can Harun al-Rashid do—come to Constantinople and demand it in person?"

"Yes, Mother," Constantine said with gritted teeth. "Harun's armies will overrun us and there will be nothing left of Constantinople but smoking ruins." He stomped out.

That evening, I had supper with Constantine. He picked at his food, moody and dark. I, too, had trouble eating. "I am going back to Prinkypos in the morning," I said. "Your mother won't change her mind about Rotrud or this bride show."

Constantine threw down his knife. "Maria of Amnia will prove to be a weak-willed, ugly creature who will let my mother walk all over her. I will refuse to wed her." He sighed. "My mother is making a big mistake by giving Adalgisos an army. Charles will crush them and invade our lands in Calabria and Sicily out of annoyance. Those are our last territories on the other side of the Adriatic Sea and my mother will lose them for us. As for her insane decision to stop paying tribute to Harun, he will come after it in person and torch every village and town along the way."

I couldn't argue with anything he said. He leaned forward and his voice grew tense and bitter. "If I am to be crowned Emperor in January, I will have to arrest

Stavrakios and Aetios and put them in prison. Then I will have to arrest my mother and send her into exile."

I struggled to find my voice. "Surely she will step down when you are eighteen and the Senate declares you Emperor."

"Oh, Auntie Thekla, your loyalty to her is equal only to your blindness to her character. Several senators have secretly assured me of their loyalty to me, and three of my trusted friends will draw their swords for me. They hate Stavrakios and Aetios with all their hearts and they want my mother gone." He lowered his voice to a whisper. "They fear what will happen to me if my mother crowns herself Empress in her own right."

I was horrified. "She would never harm you. But be careful, my dear. You will need more than three friends and the promises of senators to defeat Stavrakios and Aetios."

He nodded. "My mother's eunuchs are with her every minute. At night, she locks herself in her chambers and Aetios sleeps across the door. Or she stays in the palace she has built for herself. It is walled like a fortress and heavily guarded."

I had not seen it but I remembered Irini's words from before Constantine was born. We had been walking in the city lanes and she had pointed to an open area on the hill rising from Eleftherios Harbour. She had said, "One day I will build myself a private palace there. I will call it Eleftherios, which shares the meaning of 'freedom' and 'not married.'"

***

Constantine finally got his wish for battle. As he had predicted, when Irini stopped paying tribute, Harun al-Rashid invaded. Elias brought us the news.

"Constantine is joining the campaign against the army of the Caliphate, but not as commander; he will fight under experienced commanders."

I was terrified at the thought of Constantine in battle, but I feared even more that Irini would learn that he was plotting to arrest her and her eunuchs. Some days later, Megalo shouted for us to look over the wall. Military transport barges were docking at Pendykion. Soldiers were leading horses off the barges and setting up camp outside the town walls. A small boat was making its way towards us. It had to be Constantine. We all ran down to the harbour to wish him well. He was so handsome in his military tunica emblazoned with the symbol of his regiment that I hesitated to clasp him in my arms. But he embraced me with a smile that brought tears to my eyes, then he clasped his friends in his arms and accepted with gracious words the good wishes of the villagers. My heart swelled with pride at his strong friendships— just like his grandfather. Every year he looked more like him. Finally, we were left alone, and we went to sit with Father Dimitrios and Elias on the bench against the church. He spoke with eager enthusiasm.

"Our spies in the Caliphate say that Harun is planning to push a force up through Anatolia. We have sent instructions to the army of the Anatolia theme to try to stop him—but not to lose any men. Harun will get through them; he always does. The army of Anatolia will close in behind him and cut off his retreat. My regiment will join the army of the Opsikion theme at Malagina and attack Harun from the front."

He was so sure of success. I didn't dare think of the many battles that Harun had won. Empress Irini came out three weeks later. There was a nervous tension in her that made the chickens scatter when she booted them out of the big chair under the grape arbour.

"I am having the military dispatches from the campaign brought out here," she said, trying to get comfortable and finally pacing beside the vegetable garden. "We are a day closer to the battle and I will get the news sooner."

That was her excuse but I knew that she came because she didn't want anyone in the Palace to see her nerves. She strode the goat paths or watched Brother Grigorios on the scaffolding painting stars on the basilica ceiling. He had already covered the walls of our little convent church. Whenever she heard anyone shout that the mail boat or the imperial yacht was coming, she rushed down to the harbour. But two weeks passed with no news from the campaign.

"Constantine is deliberately not sending dispatches!" she fumed.

I had to agree. Finally, in early September, Elias brought Stavrakios out on the mail boat with a dispatch. Irini read it on the quay. Then she strode up to my study and stared feverishly at the map of the Caliphate while Sister Matrona and I watched.

"Harun's army launched the expected invasion, here," she muttered, stabbing the map. "Our armies blocked them, here. But Harun is still coming."

"We will pray for them," said Sister Matrona as she crossed herself.

And we did pray—day after day, morning, mid-day, and evening—but our prayers went unheard. Because two weeks later, Elias brought Stavrakios with another dispatch. Again Irini opened it on the quay. Her face went ashen. We stood silently around her, nuns and villagers. "Victory went to Harun," she whispered. "A bloody defeat. Constantine lost many men and officers. He is returning home with the remains of our armies."

"Come into the church and we will pray for their souls," said Father Dimitrios.

Irini ignored him and addressed Elias. "Take me to Pendykion and find me a coach to Constantinople." She and Stavrakios and her guards climbed into the mail boat.

Weeks later, Constantine's regiment marched into Pendykion and camped while they waited for the military barges to take them to Constantinople. Constantine came out to see us and we sat by the church. His shoulders were slumped with dejection.

"I am Emperor and I must accept responsibility for this disaster. My mother will call me an incompetent failure. But Auntie Thekla, I wasn't in charge. Experienced commanders made the decisions but I backed them and I accept the blame for the deaths of so many brave soldiers. Some were Palace guards before my mother banished them because they fought against her ecumenical council in Constantinople. They died fighting to defend her Empire. I grieve especially for them. Now I must face my mother's accusations of failure—and attend this bride show that she has rigged so that I must marry ugly, stupid Maria of Amnia."

"You have no choice," I nodded, sadly.

He set his jaw, like his grandfather had done. "I will follow my father's example and refuse to enter her bed, just as my father publicly refused to enter my mother's bed a month before he died. Patriarch Tarasios will have to grant me a divorce."

"People will whisper that you prefer men. And your mother won't let Patriarch Tarasios grant you a divorce."

"You will come to this absurd bride show and see how my mother humiliates me," he said. "I will send the yacht for you."

So, barely a month later, I stepped off the imperial yacht at the Palace harbour but instead of trudging up the steps to Daphne Palace, I climbed the hill to Ta Gastria convent. I couldn't face seeing a morose Constantine and a jubilant Irini. Abbess Pulkeria had a guest room available. We sat in her study and drank elderberry wine.

"The Empress has already chosen Maria of Amnia to marry Constantine," I said, as gloomy as Constantine. "I don't know why she bothers with a bride show."

"To show off her beauty, her jewellery, and her power," said Abbess Pulkeria, dryly.

I laughed, then sobered. "Constantine should be able to wed Rotrud if he wants to. In two months he will be Emperor in his own right. But Irini won't listen to him and when I try to talk to her, she accuses me of being more loyal to him than to her. It is not an issue of loyalty. He is becoming increasingly angry and resentful because of her tight control and I worry about what he will do."

Abbess Pulkeria refilled my glass. "It is difficult to be a witness. You must pay a price for having eyes. The price is that you will see what will happen and yet be unable to stop the tragedy. However painful that will be, do not allow loyalty to Irini or your love for Constantine to cloud your vision."

The next morning, I walked slowly up Mesi Street. I didn't want to see Constantine's unhappy face and Irini's smug triumph. So I delayed by wandering through the cosmetic market where I watched women brighten the blush of their cheeks with powder and draw lines around their eyes with kohl to make them pools of mystery. Beautiful women had always seemed closer to heaven than the rest of us plain-faced mortals. So, when I finally entered Chalke Gate on heavy feet, I was also curious to see what beauties the wealthy families of the Empire had on offer.

Thirteen lovelies floated from behind the scenes into the banquet room of Magnavra Palace on clouds of bright silk tunicas, their thin veils not hiding the desperate longing on their faces. Their relatives, clanking with jewellery, rubbed elbows with the dignitaries and ambassadors crowding the side tables loaded with pastries and sweets. I sampled some pastries stuffed with ground figs, apples, and sweetened lemons. I even found some stuffed with truffles.

Aetios was oozing around, bringing the candidates to speak to Empress Irini and Constantine. My heart ached for my poor boy who was struggling to make conversation. Less than a month before, he had suffered a humiliating defeat in his first battle and had returned exhausted and downhearted. Now he was having to smile at these terrified young women. Maria of Amnia was so pale, I thought she would faint. Constantine politely introduced me to her and her mother Hypatia, with a helpless gesture at Maria's numerous relatives circling him. Maria's pale lips moved without sound but Hypatia hissed proudly in my ear.

"Maria will be chosen. We have been informed."

After hours of everyone milling around like penned sheep, the Master of Ceremonies banged his staff on the floor. The room went as silent as the emperors' tombs. I could hear doves cooing in the garden. Empress Irini spoke sweetly, with her most lovely smile.

"The decision has been made. Maria of Amnia will wed my son, Emperor Constantine. The betrothal ceremony will be tomorrow. The wedding will be in November."

Sobs broke out among the rejected. The doors to the banquet room flew open and both losers and winners surged towards the tables groaning with delicacies. I left. I went to my favourite kapelarion near the Hippodrome where I treated myself to singlino—jug pork. Then I went on to Ta Gastria, feeling guilty about not going to comfort Dino but not wanting to see Irini's triumph. The betrothal ceremony the next day was in the Church of the Pharos inside the Great Palace walls. There, seventeen-year-old Irini had wed nineteen-year-old Co-emperor Leon. I watched sadly as Constantine mumbled the vows and sullenly clapped the betrothal crown on Maria's dark hair. I left before the reception.

"Maria is dull of spirit," I told Elias the next night, as we lay in his bed after a lovely seafood stew at the kapelarion and some wonderful love-making. I was tired from the ferry to Chalkidon, the night in the convent, then the walk to Pendykion. The sea breeze and autumn reds and yellows covering the hills of Bithynia had not eased my anger at the bride show and betrothal, but I felt empty. "Dino is no longer mine," I said bitterly to Elias. "In a month he will have a wife. He is terribly angry at his mother, both for forcing this marriage and for keeping him from filling even part of his role as Emperor. He swears that if she refuses to step down when he turns eighteen in January, he will have her arrested and exiled to Lesbos. He says he has friends who will help him."

Elias tightened his arms around me. "He had better have a lot of well-armed friends. They will have to pick off Stavrakios and Aetios and take on the rest of her armed eunuchs."

His words brought me no comfort.

Irini brought Maria out to Prinkypos a week later on religious retreat. She also brought Maria's mother, two sisters and several aunts. I took Megalo with me to welcome them at the quay along with Sister Matrona, Sister Evanthia, and Sister Efthia. I thought that a welcome party would help us converse with them. But even Sister Evanthia's sweet, open-hearted greeting could not penetrate their snobbery. They ignored us, except for Maria's mother, Hypatia.

"Where is the carriage that will take us to the convent?" she demanded.

"The stonemason will bring your trunks in his donkey cart. The convent is up there," I pointed. "We will walk."

They all stared in horror at the steep hill. "We cannot possibly walk up there!" gasped Maria.

"Pray to Saint Nikolaos for legs as strong as a donkey," I smiled sweetly.

"Watch how you speak to me," she hissed. "I will soon be Empress."

Father Dimitrios took them into the harbour church to thank Saint Nikolaos for their safe arrival while the five of us from the convent stared at servants unloading a mountain of baggage from the yacht.

"Three servants?" Sister Matrona exclaimed. "Six trunks? What self-indulgence!"

Maria came out of the church long after the others were in the plateia accepting flowers from the children. As we walked up the lane, she flung the flowers they had shyly given her into the bushes. I quickly retrieved them.

"What if the children find them?" I scolded. "They will be hurt."

"They are just peasants," Maria shrugged. She and her family stopped to rest so many times that Irini was out of sight by the time we entered the convent gate and crossed the pasture to the basilica.

"Empress Irini has built us a basilica," I said, opening the door. "Father Dimitrios comes once a month to give services. It would please the Empress if you light a candle."

Brother Grigorios was high on the scaffolding painting the icon of Christ Pantokrator on the inside of the dome. They dipped the wicks of our beeswax candles into the flame of the oil lamp and placed them in the sand pit. We then entered the main doors to the convent enclave and I led them into our little church in the courtyard. They stared in amazement at the icons that Brother Grigorios had painted on the walls. Maria fearfully skirted the life-size Saint Thekla on the pillar by the door, but she joined Hypatia and the others gazing in awe at the village scenes of the women saints milking goats or teaching girls to read.

It was a lovely autumn late afternoon and the sea was as purple as the mountains of Bithynia when I took them up to the imperial suite. I folded my hands and forced out my welcome speech. "Esteemed guests. These are your chambers. The entire convent is your personal retreat. You can join us in the little church in the courtyard for our regular services if you like. Empress Irini likes to walk in the gardens and feed the chickens. Whatever you want or need, I am at your service."

"I want tea and warm bread brought up here now," Maria ordered in a high arrogant voice. "The food on the yacht was inedible. I want hot water brought up for my bath. I will take all my meals here in my room. In the morning, bring first my tea, then my bath water, then warm bread with honey."

Empress Irini shrugged when I went to the study and snarled out Maria's commands. "Ask Aspasia if she can manage hot water for her bath. As for her meals, her servants can take them up to her. If she doesn't like the food, she can go hungry."

I went to Aspasia, who scowled at me. "I have no

time to heat bath water for her now or tomorrow. Let her bathe in cold water or with the nuns once a week."

I passed on the news to Maria and hid my smile at her frown.

After mid-afternoon services, Hypatia and the other women joined our meal outside at the long table under the grape arbour. They ate with us again in the refectory after evening services. Maria ate in her room and joined us only for prayers, even at dawn. A very sleepy servant came to the kitchen for her tea and porridge. Mid-morning, to my surprise, Sister Matrona and I found her in the basilica when we brought Brother Grigorios his usual hot tea and flatbread spread with honey and soft goat cheese. Maria was huddled in the far corner. She covered her face with her shawl when we walked in.

"She was weeping, poor thing," I murmured to Sister Matrona when we were outside. "It can't be easy traveling with Empress Irini."

Sister Matrona snorted. "She has always got whatever she wanted and now she is indulging in self-pity because she can't have it. She would be better off developing some strength of character. She will need it to survive the Palace."

They left a week later and we all sighed with relief.

In November, Constantine sent the imperial yacht to bring me to his wedding. It was in the Church of the Pharos inside the Great Palace, family only. Patriarch Tarasios's resonant voice echoed through the dome and the gold on his patriarchal ring gleamed in the candle-light. It was an emotional time for me. I gazed at Constantine's tall figure in the purple tunica and sleeveless long skaramangion shimmering with gold and silver thread and I saw him as an infant in my arms. My heart felt his baby heart beating against mine and my lips felt his downy baby hair. After Patriarch Tarasios finished the wedding blessings, I watched them walk in procession into the maze of Palace halls, then I caught the ferry to Chalkidon. I would see Constantine in January and watch the child of my heart be crowned, the fourth Isaurian to sit on the throne.

But January came and went with no imperial yacht. "I haven't heard even a rumour about a crowning ceremony," frowned Elias, when he came with the mail. He slid the letter I had written to Constantine into his pouch. I had asked Constantine about the coronation. "Maybe it was delayed because of the disaster in Sicily."

"What disaster? Do you mean the army that Irini sent to Sicily with Adalgisos?"

He nodded, grim. "Our army landed in Calabria just before Christmas. The Lombard dukes were waiting for them—along with an army of King Charles of the Franks. They attacked ours. It was a complete rout."

It was nearly Easter when Constantine came out to Prinkypos, a perfect spring day. Almond blossoms sweetened the breeze and flowers burst from the pastures in glorious colours. Constantine came alone, waving up at us from the yacht as it passed below the convent. By the time I got to the harbour, he was cheerfully kicking a ball around with his friends. I don't know who looked happier, them or him. He flung himself, panting, beside Father Dimitrios and me on the bench against the church and Father Dimitrios's wife brought us cups of mint tea.

"Your esteemed wife could not come?" Father Dimitrios inquired. Maria had not made a good impression the week she had stayed on the island. She had come down to the harbour once and had ignored the shy welcomes and bent knees of the women.

"The doctors say she could be with child. She feels unwell," Constantine muttered.

I could hardly believe my ears. "You're a father!"

He shrugged off my exclamation of joy. "Maria will never come here. Too primitive, she says. She spends her time with her parents and sisters. They have taken a house in the wealthy neighbourhood near the Church of Saint Irini."

"Why were you not crowned Emperor in January?" Father Dimitrios ventured. "You are eighteen; is it not the law?"

Constantine's handsome face flushed with fury. "My mother stood before the senators and advisors in the Consistory and told them that I was not ready. Stavrakios and Aetios stood behind her with her Palace guards, all armed. No one questioned her. They fear Stavrakios and Aetios." Constantine could hardly speak for anger. "Stavrakios runs the Palace. People consult him rather than me. The wealth that he has stolen is staggering." He glanced around and lowered his voice. "But he will be gone soon. My friends in the army say that the theme armies blame my mother for the disaster in Sicily. They are willing to rise against her. I am training hard with my army unit so I can join them."

"What really happened in Sicily?" Father Dimitrios asked.

"The traitorous dukes signed a pact with King Charles. Their joint armies were waiting for our ships. Our commander was cruelly put to death. I don't know what happened to Adalgisos. The brother of Patriarch Tarasios is being held for ransom. Thank God Charles didn't order them to take Sicily and Calabria while they were there. We would have lost the last of our holdings in Italy."

"How is Empress Irini taking this?" Father Dimitrios asked.

"She is blaming everyone but herself. She shouts that the Consul of Sicily knew about this pact with King Charles and didn't tell her. In the meantime, the Bulgars are crossing our border in increasing numbers and my mother is blaming the theme army of Thrace. I am planning a campaign to help them."

I beamed with pride. "You're commanding an army!"

"It is my own initiative," he said, darkly. "My mother knows nothing about it."

He spoke too soon. Mid-summer, Irini came out by herself, scowling and ill-tempered. "The Bulgar army has again invaded and the incompetent army of Thrace has let them straight in. The Bulgars killed the commander and took livestock and booty."

"Is Constantine all right?" I gasped.

"Constantine was not there," she frowned.

"But he said he was leading a campaign against the Bulgars," I blurted.

She raised her eyebrows. "Constantine has no say in military matters. I am Regent. I decide."

That November, Constantine sent the yacht for me

when Maria started having pains but Maria wouldn't let me inside the Purple Room in Daphne Palace where all imperial children are born and where I had seen my dear Constantine enter the world. My crime was having the love of her husband. I stood outside the doors listening to her screams and watching the parade of gawkers. I learned the baby was a girl by the midwife's shout.

My dear Constantine found me weeping and he brought me to see the infant drinking at the breast of the wet nurse. She placed the tiny being in my arms, knowing love when she saw it. Baby Irini was the grand-daughter I would never have. When I held her, I was holding a child of my heart.

Empress Irini stopped in briefly. "She looks like me," she announced, peering at the tiny red face peeking out of the soft wool. Constantine was even less attentive. He watched Maria and the infant be carried off in a litter to Maria's suite for the required ten days of isolation, then he beckoned me to his chambers.

"Stavrakios is finished!" he whispered exultantly. "Soon we will rid the Palace of his evil greed. We will exile him to Sicily. Aetios as well. The army hates them. Everyone in the Palace hates them. Even Irini's Palace Vigla hate him."

He sent me back to Prinkypos on the yacht. I would have preferred to cross by ferry to Chalkidon and walk to Pendykion along the sea. The clean air and a night in Elias's arms would have eased the foreboding I carried on my shoulders.

Chapter XI

In February, one month after Constantine turned twenty, the ground beneath our feet lurched and the stone walls shook as if they were being battered by siege engines. We all were familiar with the small tremors that caused little damage, but this tremor was so powerful that I was terrified it would bury us like the big tremors of centuries before that had buried hundreds of souls in Constantinople under toppling walls and burning wooden houses. Those souls received our prayers on the days marked in Father Dimitrios's calendar. I shouted for everyone to run into the pasture, far from any walls. Nuns wailed for God's mercy, chickens squawked, sheep bleated. When the earth calmed, our walls had suffered only cracks in the mortar. We ran down to the village.

Everyone was safe and inside the church. Father Dimitrios had pulled off his boots and was standing before the altar, barefooted in humility before God, praying for forgiveness for our evil deeds that had brought down His wrath. That evening, Elias sailed in to reassure us that

Constantinople was unharmed.

"Cracked houses but no fires. The city walls are intact. But Constantine is in trouble." He held out a bit of papyrus. "A courier from Constantinople brought this for you. A stranger pressed it into his hand."

I read the message aloud with horror. "Constantine is in Phiale prison inside the Great Palace! He and his friends tried to arrest Stavrakios. They failed. Empress Irini has ordered them whipped and thrown in prison. I must go there, Elias."

The crossing to Pendykion seemed forever, then the mules struggled to drag our coach slowly through the snow and mud, so it was well after dark when we pulled up in front of a pandohion in Chalkidon.

"You are my wife," Elias said, briskly pulling me inside. He took out a plump purse and demanded a private room. Soon we had a hot meal inside us and I was warming my feet against his legs in a cosy bed.

"Constantine told us that he had a plan to arrest Stavrakios and claim the throne in his own right," I whispered, staring up at the dark rafters. "How did Irini find out? Who told her? He told only me and I told only you."

But Elias was already asleep.

High winds kept the ferries from leaving Chalkidon until mid-afternoon. The wine that Elias kept pouring in my cup as we waited in the kapelarion kept my nerves calm until we got on board. I heard the captain muttering to a sailor something about wet sails and the wind snapping off the mast but by then I was vomiting over the side and I didn't care. We docked just before dusk and Elias hurried my wobbly legs through the narrow pedestrian gate beside the great Golden Gate.

"Stay off Mesi Street," a guard cautioned. "The Empress has declared an early curfew and doubled the night watch."

We kept to the deserted side lanes and arrived safely at the brothel where Elias kept a room. He had brought me there years before when I had been locked out of Ta Gastria convent after working late in Patrikia Constanta's kitchen. I had been searching in the dark rain for Aspasia's building when I had stumbled into Elias. He took me to the brothel where I slept warm and dry.

Tonight, the servants let us in swiftly. They brought warm wine, hot food, and a brazier glowing with hot coals. I spread my wet cloak over the drying rack and pulled off my boots. I lifted my icy feet towards the glowing coals while I drank down the wine and ate cabbage soup heavy with salted fish, eggs, cheese, pepper and garlic that a eunuch brought.

"People are gathering at Chalke Gate and shouting for Constantine's release," he reported in a low voice. "The army, the monks, the priests, the people—they all love Constantine. There could be riots."

Elias fell asleep but I lay beside him watching the red darkness of the brazier. "How can I get Dino out of prison, Saint Thekla?" I whispered. The answer fell into my head. Find Doctor Moses, Irini's personal physician.

The next morning, we hammered on the gate to the doctor's medical compound and his medical assistant, Andreas, took us to Doctor Moses who was having porridge in the kitchen.

"Andreas and I took blankets and food to the Chalke

Gate as soon as we heard that Constantine had been arrested," he said, grimly. "We were turned away—orders from Stavrakios. Constantine has been in a freezing cell for two nights without food or medical attention."

How Elias got us in, I don't know. One word from him and a guard hurried away, quickly to return with orders to admit us. Doctor Moses, Andreas, Elias, and I hurried to Phiale Prison where the guards were glad to open the gate. "That shit-eating Stavrakios whipped him with his own hands," a guard muttered. "It ain't right, our young Emperor, beat by a eunuch near to death."

We lit our candles from his and followed him down the dark steps. Constantine was lying on a pile of dirty straw with just his cloak to warm him. His back and arms were striped with bleeding welts. His eyes were nearly swollen shut and his fingers so mangled that he could not move them. I burst into sobs and wiped the blood off his face with my scarf. He wept when he heard my voice.

"The earth tremors destroyed our plan," Constantine groaned. "My two friends and I had got Stavrakios away from Aetios. I told him that, as Emperor, I was arresting him. We secured him with rope. Then the walls started shaking. Everyone was screaming and running into the streets. Stavrakios got away. I feared for my mother and Maria; the walls could collapse on them or fires could set Constantinople ablaze. I found them in my mother's bedchamber. I got them onto the imperial yacht and told the captain to take us up the Golden Horn to the dock below the Palace of Saint Mamas on the other side of the Golden Horn. The houses are farther apart there and there is less danger. I helped them up the steep hill. Stavrakios came with the Palace Guard. He told my mother that I was planning to arrest her and seize the throne for myself."

He moaned as Doctor Moses washed the wounds on his face. "I tried to tell her that we had arrested Stavrakios because he was amassing power and wealth. I told her that everyone hates and fears him. She wouldn't listen. Stavrakios told her to send me into exile—me, the Emperor! Nikiforos from the Finance Ministry came then and reminded my mother that it is treason to act against the Emperor. So she told Stavrakios to lock me in my chambers. She told Nikiforos that it would be just for the night. But Stavrakios brought me here and beat me with his own hands."

"I will talk to her. I will get you out of here," I sobbed.

He gripped my hands with his bloody ones. "She poisoned my father with that crown. She poisoned my grandfather with her poultice for his skin sores. She will kill me next."

I tried to speak but I could only whisper, "I will find Maria. She and I will persuade your mother to let you out."

His voice shook with bitterness. "Maria will not help me. She is afraid of my mother. So are her parents. They have probably fled home to Paphlagonia."

Doctor Moses shook his head. "Maria is again with child. She is vomiting, as she did with her first. She and her family are in their house near the Church of Saint Irini."

Elias came with me to Daphne Palace but Aetios

blocked the door to Irini's chambers. The eunuch yanked my face so near his that I smelled the wine on his breath. "Watch out, little Abbess. I could put you where no one will find you."

I heard a growl from Elias behind me, but the point of my blade was already pricking the eunuch's throat. "I will put you where everyone will slip in your blood," I hissed and pressed harder.

With a foul oath, he loosened his grip and I ran inside. Empress Irini was with Stavrakios and Theo in her map room. She cried out in relief when she saw me and rushed to take my hands. I tried to jerk them away but she hung on.

"Oh, dear Thekla. I knew you would come! Stavrakios has stopped a plot against me! My own son and three traitors tried to take the throne!"

"Not you, Empress," I said, forcing my voice to stay even. "Constantine had arrested Stavrakios. Your son was trying to protect you from him."

Empress Irini shook her head violently. "No, Thekla. Constantine came to my chambers the night before the earth tremors. He ordered me to step down as Regent. He said that he was declaring himself Emperor in his own right and if I refused to step down, he would send me to that convent on Lesbos."

"Constantine is twenty years old," I said, evenly. "He should have been sitting on the throne two years ago."

She let go of my hands and paced the room. "Constantine is not ready to be Emperor. He won't believe me. I told Stavrakios to put him under house-arrest in his chambers until I convince him to wait longer."

I gaped at her. "Empress, Constantine lies in a filthy cell in Phiale prison. I just came from there. Stavrakios beat him nearly to death."

Theo gripped my arm. "Constantine is in prison?"

I held up my blood-smeared scarf. "This is his blood. Feel it, Empress Irini! That devil standing there cut him with a whip and left him in a freezing cell with no food or blankets. Go yourself to Phiale prison and see what that brute has done to your child." I grabbed her hand and wrapped my scarf around her fingers but she pushed me away and flung the scarf on the floor, furiously wiping her hands on her tunica.

"Stavrakios, is this the blood of my son?" she demanded, her voice shrill.

"How could it be, Empress?" he smiled.

I fixed Stavrakios with my eyes and raised my right palm towards him in the time honoured way that we lay a curse. "May your tongue swell in your throat and choke you to death. May the earth refuse to accept your corpse."

The swarthy face of Stavrakios went pale and he raised his hands to block the curse, as if a curse can be blocked.

"Stop, Thekla," Irini shrieked. "Do not bring your peasant curses into my rooms!"

I shouted at her like the women in my village shout at their husbands and children. "Shame on you! Shame! You knew what Stavrakios would do when you let him take Dino away. The people of this city are at Chalke Gate calling for Dino's release. If he dies in prison, they will break through Chalke Gate and your blood will join his blood staining my scarf!"

"Get away from me!" she shrieked. "Stavrakios, take her out of here!"

I drew my knife and pointed it at him, keeping my eyes on him while I spoke to her.

"Constantine is a husband, a father, and a soldier. The army officers who helped him arrest Stavrakios are honourable soldiers who fought under Emperor Constantine and Emperor Leon. Stavrakios is draining the Treasury with his greed. He is putting his own people in high positions in the Palace. Do not punish your son for trying to protect you from him. Go yourself to Phiale prison and see the crime that devil has committed in your name."

I kept my eyes on Stavrakios through the long silence that followed. Finally Irini said, "Stavrakios, leave us."

She watched Stavrakios leave, with Theo right behind him. Then she sat down and put her face in her hands. Her voice was low and harsh.

"I was seventeen when I came to the Palace. I studied the history of the Empire and the battles fought by all our emperors. I memorized the laws written in the Ekloga. Emperor Constantine let me sit in the Consistory and Magnavra Palace and hear his decisions. I have walked down every street of Constantinople. I know every church and monastery and convent. I have toured the orphanages and hospitals and poor houses. I know how meat is butchered and where to buy the best fish. I know the price of grilled shrimp in the food stalls outside the Hippodrome. When I was heavy with child and could not go outside the Palace gates, I studied. After Constantine was born and I was forced to stay in my chambers,

I studied."

"Your son has been an equally good student, Highness."

"He has no experience in battle or commanding armies."

"Because you have not let him. Only when he was nineteen did he see battle."

"Which he bungled! I read the reports. His defeat was stupendous."

"He was not the commander!" I could not keep the anger from my voice. "He approved the decisions of experienced commanders. Yes, they lost that battle. So did Emperor Constantine lose battles."

"I cannot let him make that mistake again. I am Empress. I myself will command the army, not him."

I gaped at her. "You have no military training or experience and you will command the armies of the Empire?"

She drew herself up. "I went on campaign against the Bulgars."

"You stayed at the rear with the priests and the whores," I said brutally. "Even if you had real battle experience, no army will obey a woman—especially a woman who has plastered an icon on Chalke Gate after their beloved Emperor Constantine made them vow never to venerate icons."

Her face flushed and she shouted at me. "The army has no choice! They have to obey me as their commander."

A great sadness came over me then. My anger vanished and my heart ached at her folly. "They have a choice, Empress. They will rise against you and crown one of their own commanders. They will send you and Constantine into exile and death. The Isaurian line will end forever." I drew a breath. "Put Constantine on the throne. He has good advisors and commanders. He was born to be Emperor. Did not Emperor Constantine say so?"

She stared out the window at the darkening sea. I felt her weakening. Then I made a mistake. "And he has a wife who needs to take up her duties by his side."

Empress Irini whirled around. "That dull, ugly creature! She is trying to take my place. She barges into the Consistory and disrupts the discussions with her questions. She comes to Magnavra Palace and tells the ambassadors and petitioners that she is Empress. She is not! Constantine has not been crowned Emperor in his own right so she is not his empress. She is his consort. I am Empress! I became Empress when my husband became Emperor after his father died. He placed the crown on my head and named me Empress Augusta."

She narrowed her eyes at me. "You have become more loyal to Constantine than to me. This is treason. I could have you executed. But I won't—this time. Go to your convent. Get out of my sight." She turned her back on me.

My body went numb. Somehow I controlled my shaking voice. "Empress Irini, I vowed loyalty to you with God as my witness when you and I were eighteen. My loyalty to Constantine has not changed my loyalty to you—even after what you have done to him."

I staggered through the halls of Daphne Palace and would have fallen down the marble steps if Elias had not caught me. I collapsed into his embrace, shaking from the frightening thoughts that raced through my head. "Stavrakios told her and Theo that Dino was in his chambers. Irini thinks me disloyal," I choked. "Stavrakios has slid between us like a snake."

"Come," Elias said gently. "We will find another way to get Dino free."

Constantine was sitting up, wrapped in blankets, when we got back to the prison. His hands were bandaged and Andreas was feeding him hot soup. Constantine turned his swollen eyes on me.

"She won't let me out, will she?" he said, in quiet despair.

"Stavrakios told her that you are locked in your chambers. She believes him. I told her to come and see for herself."

"She won't," he sighed. "She wants to be Empress in her own right. She will let me die here."

"I will speak to her," murmured Doctor Moses, packing his medical bag.

Words spilled from me then, words that I had struggled not to admit but now I could not stop. "Empress Irini saved me from prison. She protected me from Empress Evdokia. She freed me from my betrothal vows and made me Abbess of an imperial convent. I believed in her clear judgment. I thought that she made good decisions. But I was wrong. Everything I believed about Empress Irini is false. Her own son believes that she poisoned his father and his grandfather. People whisper that she caused the death of Patriarch Nikitas and Patriarch Pavlos. And I have vowed loyalty to her in the name of

God." I covered my mouth to stop the horror inside me from spilling into the dark cell.

Doctor Moses spoke in a firm, quiet voice. "Irini was orphaned at a young age. She grew up among people she could not trust. Her uncle sent her with Emperor Constantine, knowing his reputation with women. She came to my clinic in Thessaloniki and I repaired her body, but her spirit was badly wounded. She was brought to the Great Palace where everyone wished her ill and she had nowhere to turn for help. She has survived by her wits and the loyalty of her cousin Theo. I am not excusing what she may have done. But she needs our loyalty more than ever. We must guide her as her trusted companions. But remember, Abbess Thekla, we cannot save her from herself. She will live or die by her own deeds—as will we all."

Theo came then with Palace eunuchs bearing pots of hot food and blankets. I spoke quietly to Theo.

"I am going to find Maria. I will beg her to come and ask Irini to let Constantine out of prison. I have nowhere else to turn," I added.

Theo answered in a low and discouraged voice. "I fear you are wasting your breath. Irini will not believe that Constantine is in prison. Her mind is only on forcing the army to vow loyalty to her."

Elias shook his head. "The army will never vow loyalty to her. Commander Tatzates and Captain Elpidios defected to the Caliph because of her and the army will never forgive her. Now she has imprisoned the legitimate Emperor and this gives them legal right to storm the Palace. We must make certain that the army raise

Constantine on their shields as Emperor—not one of their commanders."

Elias stayed with Constantine while Theo took me to the villa of Maria's parents. It was a large two-storey wooden house in the wealthy neighbourhood behind the Churches of Holy Wisdom and Saint Irini, near the villa of Patrikia Constanta where I had been a kitchen maid. Theo hammered for some time on the door before Maria's father opened it a crack and reluctantly let us inside the darkened rooms. Furniture was covered with sheets and several trunks were half-filled. Maria was lying on a couch holding her mother's hand.

"Consort Maria," Theo said. "Constantine is badly injured. He is in prison. Please come with us and ask Empress Irini to release him."

Hypatia cut in. "Why should Maria help him? Never once did he take her side against that woman. My daughter has been miserable since the day we came to this dreadful city. Empress Irini gives her one lady-in-waiting, one servant, and one nursery nurse. The baby screams all night. The food from the Palace kitchen is inedible. I have to bring her meals from my own kitchen."

I glared at her. "If Constantine dies in prison, your daughter will lose that lady-in-waiting, that servant, and that nursery nurse. She will have to return all her rich clothes and jewellery and go back to Paphlagonia."

"She will be better off than she is now." But Hypatia's eyes wavered to her daughter. Maria turned her head away and we left. I felt sick with disgust.

When we got back to the prison, Constantine was awake and eating stew that Elias was heating in a small brazier. Elias and Theo left together, to where they did not say and I was too concerned with Constantine to ask. That night, I lay next to my beloved boy, keeping him warm with my body, listening to him speak with longing of his happy childhood on Prinkypos. While he slept, I stared into the darkness. "How can I get Constantine out of prison?" I whispered to Saint Thekla. But I knew. Only Empress Irini could release him.

In the morning, I went back to Daphne Palace, heart pounding. Yesterday, Irini had accused me of being disloyal and had ordered me to return to Prinkypos. Today, she could have me thrown in prison for disobeying her order.

Aetios let me in with his usual oily sneer. Irini was in her bedchamber, combing her hair at her dressing table. She cut me off before I could speak.

"Constantine will be taken to his chambers and will remain under house-arrest until I choose to let him out."

I nodded, keeping silent. I suddenly wondered if she had known all along what Stavrakios had done.

"I have not been as lenient with the other traitors," she continued, lifting an earring to her ear and gazing in the mirror. "One has been flogged, tonsured, and exiled. The other two are stripped of their titles and are under house-arrest." She lifted her chin. "I have decided to order the army to take an oath of allegiance to me and me alone."

My heart sank. "What sort of oath of allegiance, Highness?"

"They will vow that Constantine cannot take sole power as long as I live. And they will vow to acclaim us as 'Irini and Constantine', with my name first."

"Begging your pardon, Empress," I burst out. "The army will never swear allegiance to an empress before an emperor."

She whirled around with frightening fury and flung her comb at me. It clattered against the wall, the same wall where Emperor Leon had once smashed a glass vase. "What do you know about the army?" she screamed. "You are a peasant who lies that she is a nun!"

Oddly, her violence caused a sort of calm to come over me. My words came easily and from my heart. "Highness, I know this much: Stavrakios will persuade you to appoint him head of the joint armies. Then he will arrest you and put one of his relatives on the throne. For your sake and the sake of the Empire, do not be deceived by his lies."

"Get out!" she screamed. "Go back to your convent before I lock you in prison and let you die."

That strange calm stayed with me as I returned to the prison. Constantine's personal eunuchs were carrying him out on a litter. I followed them through the snow to his chambers in Daphne Palace where the Palace physicians were waiting. Servants were bringing in braziers glowing with coals. I stared out the windows at the dark winter sea while they took him to his private bath to wash him and dress his wounds.

I stayed for many days, helping him eat, supporting his shaking steps across his bedchamber, watching his wounds heal. Theo came every day. Irini never visited and I never went to see her. The day that Maria moved back into his chambers, I left. As I walked out of Daphne

Palace, I felt no surprise to find Elias waiting. We caught the ferry across a rough sea to Chalkidon.

"How long does she plan to keep him under house-arrest?" Elias asked, as I drew a breath of the fresh air of freedom.

I lifted my hands. "A week ago, she said she plans to order the armies of all the themes to vow that Constantine cannot take sole power as long as she lives, and that they must acclaim the two of them as Irini and Constantine, with her name first. Constantine says that the army will rise against her."

"They will, but not yet," said Elias and wouldn't explain further.

I lifted my face to the sails fluttering in the icy wind. "I will remain loyal to both Irini and Constantine," I said. "But who will be first? Irini saved me from prison and made me Abbess. I vowed my loyalty to her with God as my witness. But Constantine is the child of my heart."

In Chalkidon, we caught the last coach for Pendykion and by the time we climbed off at the postal way-station, I was shaking with chills. Elias took me into the warm kapelarion and settled me on cushions by the fire. He ordered lamb stew and fed it to me. He paid for a bed in the women's dormitory, which was warm, being over the kapelarion. I was asleep even as the pandokissa was sliding a warm brick between the blankets.

The next morning, still tired, I drank a mug of steaming mountain tea and ate millet porridge. Too soon we were in the mail boat and Elias was raising the sail to catch the cold wind to Prinkypos. Aspasia, Sister Matrona, and Father Dimitrios were waiting on the quay. I clung to Aspasia's arm as I gave them the news about Constantine. I kept my arms through their strong ones up the lane to the convent. That evening, when Sister Matrona pulled on her shawl to make evening rounds, I tried to rise from my cushion in front of the kitchen hearth.

"I'll make rounds," I said, weakly. "I'm responsible for the convent."

"Stay where you are," she ordered. "A convent is responsible for itself. Believing that only oneself is responsible for the lives of others is self-indulgence."

The next morning, feeling stronger, I locked the door of my study and with trembling hands opened the secret trap door in the hearth. I lit a candle and carried it down the steep steps to the secret room. I opened the trunk that held all the wealth that Empress Irini had been bringing out since the first days of the convent. I took out the small purses, one by one, and looked inside at the gold coins and jewels.

Then I removed the big stone under the steps and lifted out the purses I had hidden there. There was the purse with that year's stipends for the nuns that I had not yet handed out. There were my own stipends that I had not spent. And there were the extra purses of coins that Irini had given me over the years. I sat down and thought. Elias had said that the army would arrest Irini; it was just a matter of time. The army might put an emperor on the throne who would not continue our stipends. Constantine and Irini might manage to escape. They would come here for Irini's treasure to buy their way into some foreign sanctuary. I would not give them all of it. I would hold some back for the convent, to keep us alive.

I reached for the trunk that held the treasure that Irini had stolen from the Palace. Then I pulled my hand back and closed the trunk. Saint Thekla had pulled me back from the brink. I sealed my hiding place with the rock.

Constantine stayed under house-arrest for eight months. I visited him for one week each month and each visit I asked Empress Irini to let him out. She always refused. Theo came every day. The second month, the Palace tailors came to measure Maria for her pregnancy tunicas. They showed her Empress Evdokia's old tunicas that they had brought to cut down for her. Maria flew into a rage.

"Irini treats me like a poor cousin!" she shouted. "When I am Empress, my first act will be to evict Irini from the Palace with only the clothes on her back, like she did Evdokia!"

After that, Maria took little Irini and moved into her parents' home. Constantine missed his little daughter but Maria's absence suited him just fine. "I am tired of her constant whining," he said. "When I am crowned Emperor, my first act will be to divorce her."

In July, the fifth month of his house-arrest, I arrived to find Constantine talking with a handsome young army officer wearing the uniform of the Palace Guard. He was as tall as Constantine and had the same open look. When he saw me, he rose to leave. Constantine held up a hand.

"Stay, Alexie. Abbess Thekla is my dearest friend. She won't tell my mother that you are here. The Abbess is loyal to me, not to her."

His words shook me because they were true. I would

protect Empress Irini; I would hide her in the convent; I would help her escape if it came to that. But I would be loyal to her only in my actions, not in my heart.

"Meet my friend Alexios," Constantine said. "My mother has appointed him as commander of her Palace Guard. She doesn't know that Alexios and I have been close friends since our army training. Every soldier who serves under his command loves him. Alexie, tell Abbess Thekla what you have just told us. Go on, my friend. Nothing you say is disloyal to my mother; it is simply the truth."

The young officer flushed from Constantine's compliments. "Empress Irini has ordered the armies of all the themes to vow loyalty to her and only her."

"Auntie Thekla, she is mad!" Constantine exploded. "No soldier will vow loyalty to a woman! Especially a woman who has imprisoned their legitimate Emperor! Alexie, go on."

The young man took a quick look around and lowered his voice. "Some of the theme armies don't want to sign. There is a sense of disregard for the authority of the crown in the Empire. The troops stationed along the Bulgar border are being lax in stopping the Bulgars from crossing our borders. We have lost life and property. Caliph Harun al-Rashid has raided Cyprus and Crete and our army there could barely stop the pillaging and push them back."

"Harun sent his naval fleet against ours in the Gulf of Attalia and they captured our commander," put in Constantine. "Stavrakios told the senators in the Consistory that the other naval commanders failed to support him."

"That was a lie!" Alexios burst out. "Stavrakios is trying to take over the army and navy! He has asked Empress Irini to hand over the command on Cyprus and Crete to his own hand-picked men."

"Soon he will go for the throne," Constantine said grimly. "The army must depose my mother and crown me Emperor before Stavrakios gets in power."

I told all this to Elias when I stayed with him in Pendykion on my way home. "You said you would protect Constantine, like Leon asked you. Why are you not protecting him? He is under house-arrest."

"There is nothing we can do at this time," he said.

"Who is 'we'?" I demanded, but he would say nothing more.

Chapter XII

In September, the seventh month of Constantine's house-arrest, Empress Irini sent the imperial yacht to bring me to the Palace. Maria was having birthing pains. I arrived to find Constantine locked in his chambers in Daphne Palace, far from the Purple Room where Maria was screaming. He was thin and pale but he grabbed my hands in joy—and not because of the coming birth of his second child.

"The army of the Armeniakon theme has refused to swear loyalty to my mother!" he shouted in triumph, whirling me around the room as he had as a child. "Alexios has just brought me the news. My mother is screaming in fury, he says. She has ordered him to go to the Armeniakon theme army and make them swear loyalty to her. Alexios was born there and his family has held high ranks in the army for generations. My mother actually believes that they will sign if Alexios gives them the order."

"What does Alexios think?" I asked, cautiously.

"Alexios says they might pledge loyalty to both me and my mother, but never to her alone." Constantine ran agitated fingers through his fair hair, so like his grandfather's. "He wants me to tell the senators to immediately name me Emperor in my own right. If I am not seated on the throne when the theme armies storm the Palace and arrest my mother, the armies could fight over whom to raise on their shields and acclaim as emperor. It could become civil war. The Caliph and the Bulgars will invade, and so will the Magyars and the Slavs. Talk to my mother, Auntie Thekla. Make her release me and let the senators crown me before we lose the throne of the Isaurians."

I understood his fear of civil war. I had overheard his grandfather telling Irini that civil war must be avoided at all costs. That evening, I went to plead with Irini to free Constantine. She cut me off.

"Thekla, I have made a decision that will settle this whole matter of a loyalty oath."

My heart leapt but quickly fell at her words. "I am sending Alexios, commander of the Palace Guard, to order the Armeniakon theme army to sign a loyalty oath to me. His family have commanded that army for generations. The other theme armies will follow their lead. Stavrakios and Aetios assure me."

I struggled to speak calmly. "Empress, why don't you ask them to vow loyalty to both you and Constantine? No army will vow loyalty to a woman alone."

She smiled. "I have replaced their commander who was a troublemaker setting the army against me. Their commander is now an officer recommended by

Stavrakios. He will order them to sign. I have done the same in other themes. I got rid of Mihalis the Dragon as well, curse the man. I have stripped him of his army rank and sent him home as a civilian. Now go over to the Purple Room and when Maria produces the next child, tell me what it is."

I did not expect to be admitted into the Purple Room and I wasn't. I waited outside the door listening to Maria scream until the midwife bellowed the arrival of a second baby girl. Constantine could not let me into the nursery to hold his daughter because he was under house-arrest. I took my time taking the news to Irini. I walked through the Palace gardens and down the steps to the sea wall where some of the huge stones had fallen into the sea. Constantine had wanted to repair them but Irini had refused. My heart ached that I could not hold Constantine's child. Tears joined the sea mist on my cheeks. Then Sister Matrona's voice came into my ears, "Weeping over rejection is just self-indulgence masked as grief."

I smiled, thinking of that powerful nun. Then a sudden terror came from nowhere and took away my breath. Since Irini of Athens had come to Constantinople, two emperors had gone to their tombs and a third sat imprisoned under house-arrest. I felt a desperate urge to go home to the grassy plains of Anatolia. I could care for my mother and father, if they were still alive. I could escape the walls of Constantinople.

Again into my ears came the strong voice of Sister Matrona. "Running away is just self-indulgence."

The terror eased. The convent was my home. I belonged where I had planted my heart. I took the news of the birth to Empress Irini, then turned my steps towards the ferry to Chalkidon and home. Alexios would protect Constantine until the armies of the themes rose up and put Constantine on the throne. Irini would turn to me to protect her. I would face my vow when the time came.

Our harvest that October was particularly plentiful. Our grapes hung heavy on our vines and the broad squash and pumpkin leaves carpeted the earth. We picked apples, lemons, pears, and quince and stored them in our root cellar. Our olives were as many as the stars. But Constantine in prison was a dark cloud in our sky. Finally, Megalo shouted that the mail boat was coming and we all dropped what we were doing and ran down to the quay, desperate to hear that Constantine was free. The sun caught the strands of silver in Elias's trim dark beard and in his long hair tied back with a leather strap. Cries of joy burst from us when we saw his smile.

"An army courier from the Armeniakon theme army came through Pendykion with news. Alexios had persuaded the theme army to vow loyalty to both Constantine and Irini—with Constantine's name first. Then the soldiers changed their minds. They have refused to vow loyalty to Empress Irini at all. They arrested the commander appointed by Irini, threw him in prison, and acclaimed Alexios as their commander. They have denounced Irini and acclaimed Constantine alone as Emperor. Army couriers are riding to the other theme armies, urging them to do the same. Alexios is marching to Constantinople at the head of an army. They will put

Constantine on the throne."

"But Stavrakios and Aetios and Irini's Palace guards control the city gates," I stammered. Even if Alexios has loyal friends inside who will open a gate, he still has to get through Chalke Gate into the Great Palace."

"There are plenty of soldiers in Constantinople who want Irini deposed. Let us pray that Alexios remains loyal and proclaims Constantine as Emperor—not himself."

"I'm going to Constantinople," I said and climbed into the mail boat. "Alexios could fail and Stavrakios will throw Constantine back in prison. I will make sure he survives."

At the Pendykion postal way-station, I hoped that Elias would get on the coach with me but couriers were galloping in from both directions needing fresh horses so I went alone to Chalkidon. I caught the last ferry to Constantinople and hurried through the pedestrian gate by the Golden Gate before dusk. It was too late to reach Chalke Gate before it closed so I went to Ta Gastria convent.

Abbess Pulkeria was standing at her doorway, observing the homeless women moving across the courtyard. I knelt and kissed the hem of her habit.

"A guest room is available," she said and motioned for me to stand beside her. I was dropping with fatigue, but I stood there until the nun closed the gate. Then I washed, prayed, and ate in the refectory with the poor women. After supper, Abbess Pulkeria sat with me in her study and listened to my news. She was not surprised.

"What a pity that Irini of Athens did not hand over the throne to Constantine when he was eighteen. Maria would be Empress but Irini would hold great power as Constantine's mother. She wouldn't have the absolute power that she holds now, but influence is power."

"Irini would never settle for influence after being Empress and Regent."

"She is a woman. She has no choice."

I slept well in that peaceful place and the next morning hurried through the markets and shops on Mesi Street to the Great Palace. What a marvellous place is a city! So much to see and eat! But I had no time to enjoy it. I had to see Empress Irini and make sure that she would not punish Constantine for the actions of the Armeniakon theme army.

Nikitas, Irini's eunuch, fetched me from Chalke Gate and took me to Irini's map room. She was glaring at a pile of dispatches that spilled across the table, tight-lipped and flushed with anger.

"The armies of the Opsikon and Armeniakon themes refuse to vow loyalty to me!" she raged as I stood in the doorway. "They have imprisoned the commanders I appointed. Alexios is marching towards Constantinople at the head of an army. Constantine incited them against me! He is a traitor! And so are you! Get out before I have you thrown in prison!"

I turned without a word and hurried to Constantine's chambers on the other side of Daphne Palace. The guards at his door were in a huddle. They eyed me nervously and opened the door. Constantine threw his arms around me.

"What has happened?" he shouted, frantically. "No-one will tell me anything." He broke down in sobs of relief when I explained that Alexios was on his way. "Alexios will take control of the Palace and raise me on his shield as commander and Emperor," he said proudly.

I was not so sure. Too much could go wrong. It would take weeks for Alexios and his army to march the length of the Empire. The Palace Guard could summon the army of Thrace for help. For ten tense days, Constantine and I lived on rumours brought stealthily by nervous eunuchs, senators, and patricians who whispered their loyalty and fled. I went out to buy his favourite street food and hear the latest rumours. At last, the guards themselves flung open his doors.

"Alexios and his army arrived at the Golden Gate and the guards opened it—for the first time since your grandfather returned from his last campaign!"

We ran to the steps of Daphne Palace where patricians and senators had gathered. They rushed to clasp Constantine by the hand and escort him to Chalke Gate to await Alexios. The guards flung it wide and then came the clatter of horses' hooves and Alexios was leaping off his warhorse and clasping Constantine in his arms, both of them sobbing with happiness. I could not stop my own joyful tears. Arm-in-arm, they marched to Irini's suite with me stumbling behind. I had vowed loyalty to Irini. Now I had to choose whether to stand with her or with Constantine.

The doors to her chambers stood wide but there was no sign of Aetios or Stavrakios. Irini was standing at the open terrace door of her map room, staring at the sea. She didn't turn when Alexios addressed her with courtesy and respect.

"Irini of Athens, I am placing you under arrest. You imprisoned the legitimate heir to the throne. This is an act of treason. You will go with us to Phiale Prison where you will remain until Constantine is crowned Emperor and he decides your fate."

"Mother," Constantine said gently. "Your reign is over. It's time to go."

She turned and, without looking at us, walked before us to Phiale Prison, ignoring all who silently watched her pass. Only when the prison guards swung open the barred door did she turn her gaze on me.

"Are you coming with me, Thekla?"

Was I? I had vowed to protect her. I should go with her down those dark steps to a damp cell. She needed me to protect her. The guards would not give her favoured treatment after what she had done to their beloved Constantine.

But my feet wouldn't move. My mouth would not speak. She waited, then with a slight smile, she walked down the steps. I heard the slam of an iron door and turned away. All I wanted was to see Constantine be crowned the Emperor that he was born to be.

With a ringing cry, Alexios shouted for his soldiers to raise Constantine on their shields. Up he went with their jubilant shouts of 'Hail Emperor Constantine'! People surged from the palaces and workshops and dropped flat in full prostration.

The soldiers lowered Constantine to the ground, then he and Alexios marched at the head of the army to Chrysotriklinos Palace. Tears of joy covered my cheeks but also tears of grief at how thin and pale Constantine looked among those muscled soldiers. My tears fell also for his mother, locked in a dark cell, unable to witness her only child claiming for himself the destiny that she had claimed for him when he opened his eyes to the candlelight of the Purple Room.

Chrysotriklinos Palace was already filled with people. People dropped in full prostration as Constantine walked proudly to the golden throne under the golden canopy of state. At the throne, he turned and faced us. Alexios dropped to his knees before him, clasped his hands on his sword hilt, and called out in a voice that echoed through the room.

"In the name of the combined armies of the Empire of the Romans of the East, I proclaim Constantine the Sixth as sole Emperor in his own right from this day forward. All hail Emperor Constantine, Hand of God on Earth." He dropped flat in full prostration, as did we all. As we rose, the Master of Ceremonies carried out the bejewelled crown resting on a purple pillow. Closely behind him strode Patriarch Tarasios, hastily pulling on a brocade robe. Behind him strode Nikiforos of the Finance Ministry, running his eyes over the crowd. For an instant, he looked at me, then his eyes slid to someone behind me and he raised his chin in greeting. I turned an instant before the person clasped me in his arms.

"Elias!" I sobbed. I would have stood there holding him forever, my heart was so full of joy, but he loosened his arms.

"Let us watch our boy become a man," he murmured.

Patriarch Tarasios reached for the crown but Alexios stepped in front of him. He lifted the crown from the velvet cushion and placed it on Constantine's fair hair. His short beard and moustache were trimmed in the same fashion as his grandfather and, at that moment, he looked so like him that I was not surprised to hear whispers that Constantine could only be that great man's son.

That glorious moment was the happiest of my life. My heart felt like it would burst. I believed that all the wrongs that Constantine had suffered in his young life would be put to right and by his own hand. I believed that my adored boy would lead our Empire into a time of peace and prosperity such as we had known under the powerful hand of his grandfather.

Constantine seated himself on his throne under the canopy of state. In a strong voice that carried easily over our excited chatter, he ordered Alexios to take his mother from prison and place her under house-arrest in Eleftherios Palace, the place of refuge that she had built for herself. He ordered that Stavrakios and Aetios be found wherever they were hiding, and that they be flogged, tonsured, and exiled to the Armeniakon theme along with all the other eunuchs of Empress Irini's household.

Constantine then ordered Alexios to find everyone banished by Irini and bring them to Constantinople to be reinstated in their former posts. First among those was Mihalis the Dragon.

Exhausted with happiness, and it being near dusk, I made my way out Chalke Gate and through the cheering crowds filling Mesi Street to Ta Gastria convent where, fortified by the wine that Abbess Pulkeria pressed into my hands, I stood in the refectory and told the women that Constantine was our Emperor.

The following day, we all went to a convent near the Forum of Constantine and stood on their upper terrace to watch our new Emperor ride in procession down Mesi Street beside Alexios on matching white chargers. At Blachernae Church, he would kneel before Patriarch Tarasios and receive his blessing. Later, I heard that the procession was so long that the drummers reached Blachernae Church before the last dignitary had left Chalke Gate.

The next day I stood in Magnavra Palace and watched my beloved Constantine sign documents, confer with advisors, and greet kneeling ambassadors who were desperate for an audience and an invitation to the banquet celebrating his crowning. He summoned all five of his uncles, who prostrated themselves before him in tears. Christoforos and Nikiforos swore that they had never plotted to seize the throne, and that Elpidios was never part of any conspiracy. They insisted that Commander Tatzates had never wanted to defect to the Caliph but that he was only trying to rid the Empire of Stavrakios.

At the end of that triumphant day, I ventured into Daphne Palace, certain that I would be turned away from Constantine's chambers, but wanting to wish him well before I returned to Prinkypos. His guards took me to him immediately. He was exhausted, exultant, and worried about his mother.

"I don't know what to do with her, Auntie Thekla. Her mute slave brought a letter from her. My mother writes that she and I can rule together. I threw it in the fire. Nikiforos from the Finance Ministry wants to strip her of her titles and exile her to that convent on Lesbos. I cannot! She gave me life. She taught me all I know of the Empire."

"She locked you under house-arrest for eight months," I said, sternly. "Keep her under house-arrest until you are confident that you can pass clear judgement on her. For now, find Stavrakios and Aetios and execute them! If you do not, they will buy an army with the gold they stole from the Treasury and one day you will find their swords at your heart."

He shook his head. "My father told me that he had learned from my grandfather never to take a life unless absolutely necessary. My grandfather did not execute Artavasdos and his sons for treason when they tried to seize the throne but rather put them under house-arrest in the Hora Monastery. And he refused to slaughter the Bulgars after they retreated from a battle."

"Your grandfather pulled back from that battle because he knew that the Bulgar retreat was an ambush. As for Artavasdos, your grandfather had him blinded and the other conspirators beheaded. The head of Vaktangios sat on a spike on Chalke Gate for three days. If your grandfather were here, the heads of Stavrakios and Aetios would already be up on spikes."

"If only I had my grandfather's strength," Constantine sighed. Then he looked at me sternly. "Stavrakios is not the only thief. My mother stole enough gold to buy an army. I saw it inside the trunk in the secret room under your study when I was a child. She will make you bring that to her so she can bribe her guards to let her escape. Go to her palace and tell her that the treasure she stole belongs to the Empire and I want it back."

"I will not let her bribe her way to freedom," I protested, even as I wondered if I could refuse her.

I had never been to Eleftherios Palace. As the guards swung open the wooden gates studded with iron nails, I remembered the day when Irini and I were both eighteen and walking through Constantinople. She had pointed to an open space on this hill overlooking Eleftherios Harbour and said that one day she would build herself a palace there. The child she had been carrying then now sat on the throne and her palace was her prison.

But what a prison! The gates opened onto lush gardens and a vine-covered archway. Birds twittered. Roses flowered in huge pots. The residence was made of white stone. Irini herself threw open the double wooden doors, with Theo behind her. I stopped, waiting for her scream of 'Traitor'. But she threw her arms around me and sobbed until Theo gently led her to a bench. She wiped her eyes.

"Theo says that Constantine has exiled all my eunuchs except for Nikitas, who is here," she said. "He tells me that some senators wanted Constantine to mutilate my eyes but Nikiforos from the Finance Ministry said that would acknowledge my legitimacy as Empress. He wants Constantine to exile me to that convent on Lesbos where everyone dies in a year. Constantine won't send me to Lesbos, will he, Thekla? Tell me that he won't."

"He says not."

She sighed in relief. "I have written to him and told him that we can rule together. He hasn't answered."

"Do not write to him," I said, coldly. "He threw your

letter into the fire and he will do the same with any more that you write."

"He wouldn't dare!" she shouted, then burst into sobs. "He will let me out! Constantine always does what I say."

I looked at Theo, who lifted his hands.

I stayed four nights in that luxurious prison with its soft couches, thick rugs, and servants polishing the brass and silver dishes. Each evening, they lit the oil lamps in every room and served food produced by a very good cook. There was even a gardener.

Theo and I went every day to Magnavra Palace to watch Constantine at work and, as we told Irini, to plead for her release. In truth, we never brought it up, we were so happy to see him taking his rightful place on the throne. Irini demanded to know what decisions he was making and the people he was meeting. She was furious that Constantine had appointed Mihalis the Dragon to head the Thrakian army. She fumed when Theo said that Constantine had appointed Yiorgios, the monk from Jerusalem, to be the personal secretary of Patriarch Tarasios.

"Yiorgios will be Constantine's spy and tell him everything that Patriarch Tarasios says and does," she spat. "Constantine never wanted me to bring back icons. He will undo everything I achieved in the Council at Nicaea."

I feared she was right.

Theodore, now Brother Theodore, arrived from his monastery in Bithynia, tripping over his monk's tunica that was too long for his stubby legs. We sat in the garden on benches warmed by the sun.

"Why did you not bring your dear mother to visit me?" Irini asked sweetly. "I miss her enriching company."

I choked back my laughter. Theodore's mother had been appointed by Evdokia to be Irini's attendant, and her unceasing prayers for Irini's soul and her praise of Theodore had driven Irini to curses. The minute that Irini became Empress, she had got rid of her. I could see how desperate Irini was for company.

Brother Theodore folded his hands piously over his round stomach. "My mother and sister have gone behind the Wall of Seclusion and I have no news. I will tell you about the plans for the consortium of monasteries that I am building." He then went on and on about the libraries and scriptoria and how he was inventing a script with smaller letters so that copying would take less time. "I will send you scrolls suitable for nuns. Even women need to enrich their minds."

"My convent already has a library and scriptorium," I yawned.

"Then I will send a monk to teach your nuns my miniscule script so you can expand your collection more quickly."

"With all your important activities, how did you find time for this visit?" I inquired.

Brother Theodore avoided Irini's gaze. "If you must know, I came to Constantinople to be ordained as a priest. My uncle, Abbot Platon, needs my help managing the monastery and I will hold more authority if I share his authority as Abbot. Patriarch Tarasios has kindly agreed to officiate."

Irini's voice went cold. "Patriarch Tarasios has time for you but no time to visit me?"

"I'm sure he'll be here soon," he stammered.

"Have you spoken to Constantine?" she pressed. "Have you told him to release me from this absurd captivity?"

Brother Theodore wiped his brow. "As yet, I have not attempted an audience with His Highness. I wish to conclude my ordination without complications. Emperor Constantine and I have never seen eye-to-eye on the issue of icons and I do not wish to argue."

He and Theo left together and Irini paced the garden, viciously snapping off jasmine blossoms and flinging them underfoot. "How long can Constantine keep me imprisoned here! I am his mother! I am Empress Augusta!"

"You kept Constantine under house-arrest for eight months and he was the legitimate Emperor," I pointed out.

She dropped onto a bench and lowered her voice. "I want you to bring some of those purses of gold coins that you have hidden under your study. I will bribe the guards to let me out. You will hire a fishing boat to take us to Kallipolis. A merchant ship will take us from there to Venice. We will go overland to the Franks. Charles will put me back on the throne."

Was she raving? I felt queasy. I had vowed to protect her but I couldn't help her escape. That would be defying Constantine.

"Constantine knows about the treasure," I murmured. "He saw it when he hid in the secret room when he was a child. He told me to tell you that he wants it back."

"Well, he can't have it," she snapped.

I said nothing and after a while she seemed to forget about it. "How is that woman's latest daughter faring?" she demanded.

"Empress Maria does not allow me to visit the nursery," I said woodenly.

"Never mind that dull creature," Irini sniffed. "I will get rid of her when I am out of here. Constantine needs sons. All Maria produces is daughters."

Patriarch Tarasios came the next day, shadowed by Yiorgios the spy. We sat in the garden with the purple autumn crocuses brightening the stone planters. "This is a veritable Garden of Eden," remarked the Patriarch with his smooth smile. "Surely there is a Tree of Knowledge somewhere!"

"You would never recognise it," I muttered under my breath. I could not forget how he had cruelly humiliated the bishops at the Council of Nicaea.

Yiorgios rested his expressionless eyes on me. "Perhaps we will find the snake instead."

Yiorgos then droned on about his cherished Saint Ekaterini Monastery in the Sinai desert and how he longed to return to its blessed silence until I wanted to scream with boredom. Patriarch Tarasios spoke little, blessing us with his silence.

I left the next morning for Prinkypos carrying a letter that Irini had ordered me to take to Constantine. Theo came with me. But when I turned down Mesi Street toward the Golden Gate and not toward the Great Palace, he smiled.

"You're not delivering Irini's letter."

"I want her to be locked up for eight months, like she locked up Constantine. I want Constantine to learn to rule without her getting in his way. You can take her letter to him. I do not wish to be their go-between." I reached into my shoulder bag.

"Neither do I. Both of them will be better off not speaking or writing to each other."

"Go home to Athens," I said gently. "Take a rest from them."

His shoulders drooped. "I would go today and be grateful to escape this mess. But Constantine asked me to stay and help him. And I don't want to leave Irini when she is so vulnerable."

"Vulnerable!" I glared at him. "Was Constantine not vulnerable when Stavrakios dragged him to a cold prison cell and beat him senseless? You said you were looking after him like a father. Why did you not rescue him? Why did you not persuade her to let him out of house-arrest for eight months?"

"She doesn't listen to me. She holds me accountable for. . .many things," he muttered.

"I hold you accountable for Constantine's safety and welfare. And do not let Irini escape. She will start a civil war." I went silent as we passed through the crowded passage next to the great arches of the Golden Gate and crossed the bridge over the stinking moat. I continued in a low voice. "She wants me to bring her gold and jewels that she has hidden in my convent. She wants to bribe her way out of the Empire."

Theo grimaced. "Irini told me to go to Kallipolis and

buy passage for the two of us on a merchant ship that will take her to Venice." He gave me a steady look. "Constantine would not punish us. Pope Adrianos and Charles of the Franks won't help her get back in power. They don't like women occupying a throne. They want Constantine and our armies standing between them and the Caliph."

We were at the ferry dock and I was holding out my coin to pay passage when a monk stepped forward and waved at a nearby fishing boat. "Abbess Thekla, your private vessel awaits."

"Elias! You waited here for me!" I smiled in relief.

"And for Constantine, had Alexios not arrived in time. We couldn't let him be imprisoned again, could we, Theo?"

Elias clasped Theo's hand, boosted me into the boat, and climbed in himself. As the boat eased out into the waves, our eyes moved to the line of naval vessels moored outside the Palace harbour gates.

"The naval officers are inside the Palace, pledging allegiance to the Emperor," said Elias. "Constantine would be wise to travel to every theme and secure oaths of loyalty from all the armies. He is only four years younger than his grandfather when he took the throne, but he has only one battle under his belt. He needs campaign experience before his commanders will trust him. Until then, he will have to gain the loyalty of his troops with his considerable charm. How long does he plan to keep his mother under house-arrest?"

"He doesn't know."

"Let us hope that it is a good long time. The army will

not trust him if he is lenient with her."

I took from my pocket Irini's letter to Constantine and slid it into the sea.

That winter, I did not visit Irini as diligently as I had visited Constantine. I wrote letters but there was little to report except to describe the patients in Sister Efthia's hospice, the progress of the village girls taught by Sister Evanthia and Sister Filothei, and the rugs growing on the nuns' looms under Sister Matrona's watchful eye. The little mail boat came in good weather but Elias was never at the helm when I went down to give the courier my letters for Irini and Constantine.

"Where's Elias?" I demanded, the first time he didn't appear.

"Gone on some journey," he shrugged.

My irritation with Elias for not telling me that he was leaving or where he was going added to my worries about Constantine and how he was handling his duties. I heard nothing from Constantine or Irini.

"She will want me to come to Constantinople to keep her company," I complained to Sister Matrona as we were going over the accounts.

"Worrying about the future is a waste of time," she said sternly. "You are needed in the present."

Winter passed and Lent came and neither Irini nor Constantine had written. Near Easter, the imperial yacht arrived with Theo on board. We sunned ourselves on the bench by the church with Father Dimitrios. His eldest daughter brought us thyme tea while he rocked the cradle of his latest son. Through the open door of his cottage, I could see the small icon of Saint Nikolaos perched on the icon shelf by the door and the icon of Saint Paraskevi on a stand on the kitchen shelf. Constantine had made no proclamations about icons as yet, but I could not forget his words condemning them as idols.

Theo pulled out a rolled-up papyrus and handed it to me. "From Irini. Constantine is blocking her mail so she made me bring it."

"Why is he blocking her mail?" I was surprised.

"The postmaster in Constantinople brought him letters that Irini's mute slave had taken to the postal station. Irini was writing to all sorts of people, begging them to rescue her. She wrote to Elpidios in Africa, absurd after she drove him to defect to the Caliph! She wrote to Charles of the Franks. She even wrote to Pope Adrianos. Constantine was furious."

I opened the letter and sighed. "She orders me to come. We don't start planting until April so I have to go."

"Take plenty of money from the treasure she hid out here." He smiled at my surprise. "I always knew that she was looking after herself." He sobered. "She needs it for her household expenses. Constantine gives her nothing."

"How long does he plan to keep her under house-arrest?" Father Dimitrios asked.

Theo lifted his hands. "One day he tells me that she will stay there indefinitely. The next day he says he is going to exile her to Lesbos."

I went up to the convent, put Sister Matrona in charge, and took a purse of coins from the chest in the secret room.

Our sunny March day had gone cold by the time Theo and I got to Irini's palace and I was chilled. But it was colder inside than out. Irini was wearing her fur boots and fur-lined cloak and huddled on a couch in front of a brazier scarcely warmed by a few coals. Her face was thin and her hands were icy when she clutched mine.

"Constantine wants me to freeze to death," she complained, hoarsely. "He sent me here with only the clothes on my back and a small trunk that my slave managed to pack."

"That's more than you allowed Empress Evdokia," I said. Still, my heart felt a stirring of sympathy.

"Evdokia was no longer Empress. I am still Empress Augusta. Constantine has not revoked my titles. Yet he sends me nothing to pay my expenses. My staff have left. I have no money even for food or charcoal or wood. Constantine won't let me send letters so I can't even write people for help. My slave goes to Ta Gastria convent every day and brings back our food for the day. I have never eaten so many beans. Did you bring a purse of coins?"

I started to untie the leather purse from around my neck but she stopped me. "Go now and buy food and fuel. I have nothing in the house even for a mouse."

Her mute slave and I bought cooked lamb stew for supper, millet flour and eggs, and a bag of charcoal for the brazier. Theo was gone when we returned and Irini was sitting in the dark. The slave got the charcoal going and we ate by its warm glow.

"Tomorrow I will order oil for the lamps," I said.

"And a load of wood and charcoal and a supply of candles. The servants stole it when they left, unpaid. I don't blame them." She mopped up the last of her stew

with her bread. "Theodore has not visited since he became Abbott. He writes long letters but I have to wait
a long time between them because Constantine reads
them at his leisure. Theodore advises me to pray. For
what? Will God bring me drinking water and charcoal?
Fanis has not written a single letter. Patriarch Tarasios
came only twice trailed by that spy Yiorgios so we can
say nothing that we don't want Constantine to know.
Doctor Moses comes only when my slave tells him that
I am ill. Where are all the people who ate their meals in
my reception room? Hilarion, my tutor, is my only loyal
companion, but then he is being paid. He brings me
scrolls and codices and sausages wrapped in flatbread.
But nothing interests me. Did I ever have real friends,
Thekla?"

"Theo has not abandoned you."

"He comes every few days and leaves quickly. I am
being ostracized, just like the Athenians ostracized Euri-
pides and Pericles. The ancients knew the terror of being
shunned."

"You placed Constantine under house-arrest for eight
months," I said, feebly, knowing what she would say.

"He had visitors. And his wife, such as she is. And
he was in the Palace with hot coals in the braziers and
hot food from the Palace kitchens. Oh Thekla, I so miss
Athens and the pillars of the Temple of Athena and the
statues of philosophers on the street corners. If Constantine would only let me go home to Athens. Theo will take
me and you will come. We will sail down the Aegean;
you can't imagine how beautiful are the islands rising
from the sea mist. Thekla, go now to the Palace and beg

Constantine to let me come and plead for my release."

Athens! Irini had told me so much about that ancient city that I could practically smell the olive groves. But my heart hardened. She only wanted me to bring her to Constantine so she could persuade him to let her out. She would never take me to Athens.

The next day, she had a surprise visitor—Empress Maria with little Irini who was just walking, and four-month-old Efrosini in her nurse's arms. Two servants followed, bearing a loom.

"You can weave away the hours," Maria said with a cruel smile on her fleshy lips.

I didn't hear Irini's retort because I was clasping Efrosini in my arms. Her tiny fingers wrapped around mine and she looked up at me with her big innocent eyes. I sat on the rug and held her in my lap while little Irini showed me her doll.

Empress Maria was plump and pink with health. Long emerald earrings brushed the collar of her full-length lynx coat that was open to show a long green wool tunica and red boots. A gold chain with a large ivory cross decorated her thick neck and her fingers sparkled with rings. Irini looked her over coolly.

"You have been foraging in my closets. Do not assume that what is mine is yours. I will be back."

Empress Maria smirked. "My husband told me that he is sending you to Lesbos. I am Empress now. I sit with him in Magnavra Palace and I speak to his advisors in the Consistory. Ambassadors come to my reception."

"He hasn't named you Augusta. Leon named me Augusta as soon as he crowned me Empress."

"Leon also said he would never again sleep in your bed."

Irini's voice was cold. "I was Empress before you came and I will be Empress after you are gone."

Maria slid her acid smile around the room. "This doesn't look like the Great Palace to me." She yanked Efrosini from my arms and slammed the door behind her.

"Stupid woman!" Irini fumed. "I will get rid of her like I got rid of Evdokia."

"You are baiting a wolf," I cautioned.

"She lacks a wolf's intelligence. Go now to the Palace. Tell Constantine that six months of house-arrest is enough. And bring me my jewellery before that fool woman finds where I hid it. You know the place."

"The hole behind the tapestry in your bedchamber."

"And bring me some grilled shrimp from the place by the Hippodrome."

Escaping with relief, I smiled at her absurd demand that I retrieve her jewellery from Maria's bedchamber. I couldn't possibly get inside. And the jewellery belonged to the Empire. Irini only wanted it to bribe her way to freedom.

I strolled up Mesi Street smiling at the vendors calling out their wares and breathing in the familiar aromas of cooked food. I spent a coin from Irini's purse on a pastry filled with nuts and honey. Then I bought a wagonload of wood, a case of charcoal, four barrels of fresh water, and two barrels of good wine, to be delivered to her door. The merchants remembered me from when I had shopped for Ta Gastria convent and they promised quick delivery. At Chalke Gate, the guards also remembered me and sent me to Daphne Palace without an escort. Constantine was in his chambers, resting. He threw his arms around me and led me to a couch. He shouted for a eunuch to bring sweetened kitron juice.

"You look well," I stammered, self-conscious in the presence of this handsome, energetic man with an air of authority. He gripped my hands tightly.

"Auntie Thekla, I would be dead if you had not brought Doctor Moses to the prison after Stavrakios nearly killed me. You cared for me in prison and when my mother put me under house-arrest. Now she writes me letters begging for her freedom."

"Send her to Prinkypos," I said, impulsively. "I will read any letters that come for her and any letters she writes. She can't leave the convent because the villagers will stone her—they are so angry about what she did to you."

He smiled and shook his head. "Auntie Thekla, she will twist you around her finger. In a week, she will be at the court of Charles of the Franks talking him into putting her back on the throne."

I flushed, ashamed that he knew how powerless I was against her, yet proud that he knew the strength of my loyalty. "At least, give her an allowance for food and fuel. You had every luxury when she put you under house-arrest. She is cold and hungry."

His face hardened and he looked just like his grandfather. "She has the purses of coins and jewellery she stole from the Palace. Use them to buy her food." He held up his hand. "We will not speak of my mother. I have more important things to consider."

He stood in front of the wall map of the Empire—Irini's map—and stabbed it with his finger as she used to do. "We live in a time of great empires. To our east lies the Caliphate, to the north are the Bulgars, the Khazars, and the Magyars. The Slavs sit along our western border. The Franks are farther away, but Charles only thinks of expansion. He is my mother's age and still strong. He has buried three wives and taken a fourth. He has an alliance with Pope Adrianos that gives him control over the papal territories."

His finger traced our long border with the Caliphate. "My ambassadors tell me that Baghdad rivals Constantinople in magnificence. My grandfather tried to make peace with them. He sent our builders to teach them how to construct buildings to the height of our churches. He sent our artisans to teach them about mosaics and glass design. Yet Caliph Harun al-Rashid continues to send his armies over our borders and take booty and prisoners. He is only five years older than me but his skill in military tactics far surpasses mine. His army is fanatically loyal to him and my commanders warn me that we cannot win in open battle. We cannot even stop him from invading; our borders are too long and our armies spread too thin. All we can do is ambush them when they come over the border and harass them until they leave. We cannot afford to lose one soldier; they have families to feed and fields to till. I must find another way to live in peace with our neighbours."

He threw himself on the couch. "I dream of building an Empire that is more magnificent and powerful than all of them, but I don't know how. My grandfather died when I was five and my poor father died when I was nine, so I learned little from them. My grandfather ruled for twenty-five years and his father ruled for thirty-seven years. If only I could rule that long, and with their wisdom. Now that my mother cannot interfere, I am going to try."

My heart overflowed with love and admiration for this young man I had known since he opened his eyes to the candlelight of the Purple Room. I could have sat there forever listening to his ideas, but his advisors came and I went out to the markets to buy food for Irini. In the big market behind the Church of Holy Wisdom, I bought flour, dried beans and lentils, squash, carrots, and apples. In the meat market, I bought cooked sausages and a tin pot of rabbit stew. When I got back, the deliveries had arrived. The mute slave heated the stew on the brazier and Irini quickly devoured it. Then she sat back and ranted. She had always been suspicious of everyone, but now she accused people of plots more devious and malicious than could be true. Constantine was the centre of her wrath. She criticized his appointments for every post, his foreign policy decisions, even the order of seating at his banquets. Nikitas her eunuch was her informant for that.

"Constantine doesn't appreciate anything I have done for him—I who gave him birth and taught him everything he knows. Watch, he will be unable to make a single good decision without my advice."

That night, I fell asleep to the light of her candle and the scratch of her pen on papyrus. In the morning, after our breakfast of warm flatbread that the mute slave made over the brazier and that we filled with heavy goat cheese and honey, she gave me a canvas pouch.

"Take these letters to the Jews in the Copper Market and pay whatever they want to deliver them."

When I was some distance away, I opened the pouch. I gasped at the names written on the letters and stamped with Irini's seal into red wax: Caliph Harun al-Rashid, King Charles of the Franks, our own Consul of Sicily, Pope Adrianos, the three Patriarchs of Antioch, Jerusalem and Alexandria. I sat on a stone step for a long time deciding what to do. In the end, I did what she wanted. I went to the Jewish quarter.

Years before, I had gone with Irini and her attendants into the Church of the Virgin of the Copper Market which is in the Jewish quarter. The church had once been a synagogue, I had been told. Irini had knelt before the casket containing the Veil of the Virgin and prayed to be with child. Afterwards, we had wandered through the narrow streets where the Jews lived and worked, and peeked into the shops selling elegant jewellery and leather goods. Now, after getting lost many times, I finally came upon the shop where Irini had purchased a ring. The owner must have recognised me for he let me in quickly and locked the door. I handed him the letters.

"Can you arrange for these to be delivered? You know who these are from," I said.

He read the names and shook his head soberly. "These will take months to deliver and I can't guarantee that they will arrive."

"I don't care if they end up in the sea. I want them out

of my hands." I untied Irini's purse from the cord around my neck and counted out the coins.

I then went to the Church of the Virgin of the Copper Market and stood before the barred niche that held the Veil of the Virgin. "Please let those letters reach their proper destinations—even if it is the bottom of the sea," I prayed. The next day I went home to Prinkypos.

Elias returned in May, without explanation. His beard was shaved and he had a tonsure, meaning he had been disguised as a monk.

"Are the Empire's abbotts still abusing their monks?" I queried.

"If they can get away with it." He looked tired but his smile was as cheerful as ever.

"What are you really doing, and who for?" I demanded.

"Assessing the mood of the Empire for my Emperor."

I wanted details, but he would say no more. That week I went again to Constantinople. Aspasia went with me. She wanted to see her family and I was glad of her company, although I would have spent the night with Elias if she hadn't come along.

Irini had been under house-arrest for over seven months. She and her mute slave were sitting in the overgrown garden; it had gone wild without the gardener. Inside, the elegant dining table was covered with scrolls and codices. Irini dropped onto a couch.

"The army has suffered only defeats since Constantine locked me in here. Last month he went off on another useless campaign against the Bulgars. Our army was forced to retreat. At least we lost no land and only a few soldiers. This summer, he will go against Harun when the Thief of Baghdad invades our border. Constantine will do no better than he has against the Bulgars." Her smile of satisfaction shocked me.

"I will pray for his success," I said, angry at her sneers.

She yawned. "God does not choose sides on a battlefield; ask any seasoned soldier. Pray for a good commander. Thekla, talk to Constantine. Tell him to let me out. Seven months is enough punishment."

The guards at Chalke Gate directed me to Chrysotriklinos Palace, where I found Constantine receiving a group of foreign ambassadors with easy grace. He nodded to me but there was no time for even a word. I left feeling happy that he was doing well.

I stayed with Irini for a week, stocking her larder and her wood and charcoal bins using the coins in the purses she had hidden under my study. She had no visitors but Theo who came every day and irritated her with his praise for Constantine. After seven days, I went home, relieved to be outside those prison walls. Aspasia and I took the early boat to Chalkidon. The twenty-mile walk to Pendykion passed quickly in the lovely May weather. We arranged for beds in the convent dormitory, then had supper with Elias in the kapelarion.

"Constantine wants to be like his grandfather and great-grandfather," I smiled, so proud of him and happy to show it instead of hiding it from Irini's wrath. "The army loves him and the people love him. He is full of ideas and plans."

Elias didn't share my smile. "He lacks the strength of character of those two great emperors, I fear. Certainly he lacks their military and administrative skill. He's had so little training or experience that he must rely too much on his advisors. He needs a success on the battlefield before he will gain the love of the army and the people. They want to see him marching prisoners up Mesi Street."

"He also needs to do something with his mother besides keeping her under house-arrest," commented Aspasia, scooping more sea bass from the platter onto her plate.

I sat back, still hungry but too tired to eat. "These trips to Irini are exhausting," I sighed. "If he would let her out, I could stay home."

Aspasia looked at me sharply. "Whether she is locked up or free, you cannot keep leaving the convent for long periods. We worry about your safety and this saps the strength of the nuns. Everyone is irritable while you are gone. The novices complain that Sister Matrona is working them too hard. Megalo needs new bed straps but she can't manage to weave them and no one will help her. And the village carpenter hasn't repaired our shutters."

"Stop visiting Irini," Elias said sternly. "She has got what she deserves. Your convent needs you more than she does."

Chapter XIII

That October, Irini and I were both thirty-nine and she had been under house-arrest for one year. I arrived in Constantinople to find the once lavish rooms empty except for one couch pulled near a cold fireplace.

"Are you bringing me money?" Irini lashed out in a high angry voice. "I had to sell my furniture for food and wood. My slave is back to bringing our meals from Ta Gastria. She carries our water from the public fountain. I can't remember when I last had a hot bath."

She was so thin that she seemed to float, like an angel in one of Brother Grigorios's icons. It was dusk and the markets were closed but I went out and bought grilled shrimp in a kapelarion and we ate them in the garden. She stared into the shadows as if she were seeing something I could not.

"Sometimes I feel that I have passed through the veil without ever dying," she murmured so softly that I had to strain to hear. "The ancients believed that at death we descend to an underworld where we can see the past. I believe that I already go to this place. My eyes are open and yet I can see my mother and father, just as I see you. I see Leon with his ragged beard. Emperor Constantine comes to my bed. Do not look alarmed, Thekla, it is a comfort to feel his great body warm against mine. I lie in his arms and I feel the joy of the first time, the exhilaration, and oh, the triumph."

I was so horrified that I could scarcely draw breath. "Highness, these people are not real. You are dreaming."

"Oh, they are very real." I could feel her smile in the dark. "They are as real as the shadows in this garden. But I know they should go. They muddle my thinking and I need to keep my wits about me. Ask Saint Thekla to send them away. Particularly Leon. He wanders through these rooms with his unhappy face and his annoying cough and disturbs my peace."

She added wine to all our cups; the mute slave was eating and drinking with us. "Leon had eunuchs in his bed. Everyone knew," she went on in a more practical tone. "I didn't care; I had given him the heir to the throne and that was enough for both of us. Leon had Anastasios from the Senate in his bed, and the eunuch who was in charge of the Great Palace buildings. That same eunuch used to unlock the door to my chambers to let Elpidios in after dark. Leon also had Vasilianos and Giorgios, and others. I lost count. Now, Leon brings them into my bedchamber. Tell me, Thekla, why does he come to my bedchamber now when he wouldn't when he was alive?"

"The dead will have their vengeance."

She misunderstood. "Poor Leon; he was punished enough, losing his mother at birth and growing up under that giant of a father."

"You must not allow your eyes to see these ghosts."

"Ask Saint Thekla to send them away. They won't listen to me."

The next day, I went to visit Doctor Moses. "She is seeing ghosts."

He was not surprised. "It is the result of too much solitude. There is no remedy but company."

For that reason alone, I wrote to Theodore at his monastery. It was a mistake, as I learned soon enough. It is never good to interfere in another person's life, even with the best of intentions. We each make our own fate. When I look back, I see how my interfering set the whole disaster in motion.

"Irini needs company," I wrote to Abbot Theodore. "She values your conversations. Please visit."

When I returned in November, Abbot Theodore was there. And standing demurely beside him was a frighteningly beautiful and very young girl who was as graceful as a doe. She seemed familiar.

"Tula," Irini introduced her with a smug smile. "Abbot Theodore's cousin. His mother brought her to my chambers a few times. She is my new lady-in-waiting."

"Lady-in-waiting?" I exclaimed and stared with disbelief at the beautiful child standing before us with her dark eyes turned modestly downward and a long dark curl brushing her rose-blushed cheek. Her calm features held a certain dreamlike sweetness. Then I remembered her. Theodore's mother had brought her to the Palace when she was barely eight years old. Everyone had gone silent in the face of that innocent perfection. Now she had an added quality—sensuality. With the lift of an eyebrow, this girl could turn a man to mush.

"How old are you?" I demanded.

"Twelve years, Abbess Thekla." Her voice was as soft as a cat's purr.

Abbott Theodore was beaming and rubbing his chubby hands together with satisfaction. "I persuaded Constantine to visit his mother today. Over a year of separation—disgraceful, I told him."

"One year and three months," Irini corrected, watching me with a secretive smile. Then I heard Constantine's voice in the garden and I knew what Irini was plotting. I knew why beautiful Tula was there.

Constantine walked in the door and his eyes fell on the lovely girl wearing a clinging silk tunica that showed every line of her curvy body. Instantly, he was lost. She dropped gracefully to the floor in full obeisance. Stunned, he raised her with his hand and gazed into her large dark eyes. While Abbott Theodore droned on about his monkish projects at his monastery, Constantine's eyes followed Tula. She poured him a glass of wine and her slim fingers touched his.

"What a pity that you are so long separated from your dear mother," she murmured in her husky voice.

His eyes did not leave her face. "Truly a pity," he stammered, in a trance.

Hours later, I walked him to the gate. He had spoken to only Tula. His eyes turned to the doorway where she was standing beside Irini. She bowed her head gracefully.

"When are you making a decision about your mother?" I demanded, furious with him for not meeting my eyes.

"I will let her out. She has suffered enough," he said, with his eyes on Tula.

I wanted to shake him. "Do not be distracted by this child!" I snapped. I could hear the desperate urgency in my voice.

"I am going to marry her." He lifted a hand to her in farewell.

I left a week later, when the disaster was complete. The beautiful Tula was living in Constantine's imperial suite in Daphne Palace and sleeping in his bed. Empress Maria and his two little daughters had been forcibly moved to the other side of Daphne Palace. And Empress Irini was packing to move back into the Great Palace.

I sat on the ferry to Chalkidon, watching the waves crash against the shore as we pulled out of the harbour. I turned my gaze downward into the deep blue water and felt my thoughts deepen and become clearer. Irini had got what she wanted. She would soon be back in the Great Palace bearing her titles of Empress Augusta and sitting on her throne by Constantine's side. She had done what she needed to do, to get what she wanted.

Constantine, too, had got what he wanted. He was now Emperor in his own right, and he had got rid of Maria, as he had said he would do the year he was married. He intended to marry the twelve-year-old girl lying beside him in his bed. She was barely ten years older than his daughter, and not old enough for a legal marriage. Constantine would have to persuade Patriarch

Tarasios to approve a divorce from Maria who had done nothing wrong to deserve such humiliation.

I lifted my eyes from the blue water and traced the white line of road from Chalkidon along the sea to Pendykion. Where was my mysterious Elias and what was he doing? Would I find him at Pendykion when I got there, lifting bundles of mail from the saddlebags of tired horses? Would I find comfort in his arms in his room over the wheelwright? Or would he have left on some mission whose purpose he would hide from me? He had told me that he had vowed to protect his childhood friend, Emperor Leon. But he had failed horribly and Leon had died in agony from a poisoned crown which now hung on the wall of the Church of Holy Wisdom, never to be touched again, on Irini's orders. The pain of Elias's failure hung on his shoulders; I could see it. He had told me that he had transferred his loyalty to Constantine and had appointed himself the young Emperor's protector. But Elias was still postmaster in Pendykion, a day's journey to Constantinople. How could he protect Constantine? He had said he had a confederate inside the Great Palace, and once he had mentioned Nikiforos in the Finance Ministry, but what did an accountant have to do with protecting Constantine?

I shifted my gaze to the green mountains of Bithynia and my thoughts turned to myself. I also had got what I wanted. Constantine was on the throne and Irini was out of house-arrest. But at such a cost! A coronation that should have happened easily and with joy when Constantine was eighteen had taken three years of struggle and Irini and Constantine had locked each other under house-arrest. Now they sat side-by-side on the thrones of Emperor and Empress. How long could that possibly last? Since Irini had arrived in Constantinople, two emperors and two patriarchs had died suddenly four years apart. I had seen it with my own eyes.

I heard the voice of Abbess Pulkeria in my ears. "You must pay the price of having eyes," she had said. Now I understood. The price is memories. We pay for witnessing the acts of others in the memories that we cannot forget, no matter how hard we try.

A terrible war was coming between Irini and Constantine, I could feel it. They were equal in power now, and the winner would rule the Empire of the East. The time had come for me to choose to whom I would pledge my loyalty. One cannot fight on both sides of a battlefield; one must choose who is friend and who is foe. To stand in the middle is to be attacked by both sides. Did I stand and fight for Irini of Athens? She had lifted me from peasant girl to Abbess of an imperial convent and demanded that I vow loyalty to her above all others. Or did I stand and fight for my beloved Constantine? He was the child I never had, the child of my heart.

***

The Empress Irini Series

Book 3:
Seizing Power

In order of appearance. *Fictional characters are in italics.*

Irini of Athens – Born in Athens, orphan raised in the house of her uncle, taken by Emperor Constantine V by warship to Constantinople to marry his son, Leon, becomes Empress Regent for her only son, Constantine, after the deaths of her father-in-law and her husband.

Thekla of Ikonion *– Travels to Constantinople from Ikonion and becomes the abbess of the Convent of the Theotokos on Prinkypos Island near Constantinople renovated by Empress Irini for her retreat. Based on a nun who lived in a convent near Constantinople and wrote hymns.*

Elias *– Travelling companion of Thekla of Ikonion, from a wealthy Constantinople family, postmaster in the seaside fortress of Pendykion.*

Theo – Based on Irini's cousin Theophylaktos who accompanied her to Constantinople.

Emperor Constantine V – Emperor of the Roman Empire of the East, powerful military commander and skilled administrator.

Emperor Leon – Son of Emperor Constantine V and his Khazak princess first wife, husband of Irini of Athens, father of Constantine VI.

Emperor Constantine VI – Only child of Emperor Leon and Irini of Athens, becomes emperor at the age of nine after the death of his father, called 'Dino' in the book.

Princess Anthusa – Only daughter of Emperor Constantine and Empress Evdokia, twin sister of Prince Christoforos.

Empress Evdokia – Third wife of Emperor Constantine V, mother of five of his sons and one daughter.

Empress Maria – Based on Maria of Amnia, first wife of Constantine VI

Baby Irini – Based on Irini, first child of Constantine VI and Maria of Amnia.

Baby Efrosini – Based on Efrosini, second child of Constantine VI and Maria of Amnia.

Empress Tula – Based on Theodote, second wife of Constantine VI.

Alexios – Based on Alexios Mousele, loyal friend of Constantine VI.

Megalo – Based on the daughter of Patrikios Leon and Patrikia Constanta, married to Fanis, lives in the convent on Prinkypos Island.

Fanis – Based on Theophanes the Confessor who married Megalo and became a monk.

Patriarch Pavlos – Based on Paul of Cypress, Ecumenical Patriarch appointed by Emperor Leon.

Patriarch Tarasios – Based on Tarasios, Ecumenical Patriarch appointed by Irini of Athens.

Abbess Pulkeria – *Abbess of Ta Gastria convent in Constantinople.*

Aetios – Based on Aetios, eunuch guard for Irini.

Stavrakios – Based on Stavrakios, eunuch guard for Irini.

Patrikia Constanta – *Based on the wife of Patrikios Leon and mother of Megalo.*

Patrikios Leon – Tax official in the Great Palace, father of Megalo.

Mihalis the Dragon – Based on Michael Lachano-drakon, military commander under Emperors Constantine V, Leon, Constantine VI and Empress Irini.

Tatzates – Based on Tatzates, military commander under Emperors Constantine V, Leon, Constantine VI, and Empress Irini.

Bardanes Tourkos – Based on Bardanes Tourkos, military commander under Emperors Constantine V, Leon, Constantine VI, Nikiforos I, and Empress Irini.

Doctor Moses – Based on physician by that name living in Antioch in the Caliphate.

Abbott Theodore – Based on Theodore the Studite.

Elpidios – Based on Elpidios, military officer accused of having an affair with Empress Irini.

Father Dimitrios – *Village priest on Prinkypos island.*

Brother Yiorgios – Based on George Synkellos, monk historian.

Caliph al-Mahdi – Leader of the Caliphate during the reign of Emperor Leon and Empress Irini.

Caliph Harun al-Rashid – Leader of the Caliphate during the reigns of Empress Irini and Emperor Constantine VI.

Nikiforos – Based on Nikiforos, Minister of the Finance under Empress Irini of Athens.

Pope Adrianos – Bishop of Rome (pope) and ruler of the Papal States for 23 years.

Princes Nikiforos, Christoforos, Nikitas, Evdokimos, Anthimos – Sons of Emperor Constantine V and Evdokia, half-brothers of Emperor Leon, uncles of Constantine VI.

Sister Efthia – Nun at the Convent of the Theotokos on Prinkypos Island, directs the hospice.

Aspasia – Cook at the convent of the Theotokos on Prinkypos Island.

Sister Evanthia – Nun at the Convent of the Theotokos on Prinkypos Island, teaches the village girls their letters and numbers.

Sister Matrona – Ekonomis, second in command at the Convent of the Theotokos on Prinkypos.

Sister Filothei – Teaches the village girls their letters and numbers.

Auntie Sofia – Aunt of Elias, lives in Nicaea.

Adalgisos – Son of the King of the Lombards, takes asylum in Constantinople.

Brother Grigorios – *Monk who paints icons on Prinky-pos Island*

King Charles of the Franks – Also known as Charlemagne.

Rotrud – Daughter of King Charles of the Franks

Note: The EMPRESS IRINI series covers the years 752 AD – 803 AD. During this time these people called themselves Romans of the East. They are now called the Byzantines.

Biographical data is available at http://www.pbe.kcl.ac.uk/data/index.html, Prosopography of the Byzantine Empire.

Glossary

Aegean Sea – body of water between mainland Greece and Turkey

Amorion – fortified Roman city in Anatolia and large military base

anagrapheus – tax official

Anassa, Amma – terms of respect for an abbess

Anatolia – Large theme in the centre of the Empire of the Romans, now central Turkey

Antioch – wealthy city in the Caliphate

artopios – bread vendor

Akimiti monks – monks who never sleep so they can continually pray

Augustaion – large area between the Church of Holy Wisdom and the Great Palace

biblioamphiastis – bookbinder

Bithynia – rich farming area near Constantinople

Blachernae Palace – Imperial Palace in Constantinople on the Golden Horn, said to have the Veil of the Virgin Mary

Bosporus Straits – narrow waterway connecting the Propontis Sea and the Pontus Sea (the Sea of Marmara and the Black Sea)

Caliphate – empire east of the Roman Empire of the East

Chalke Gate – entrance to the Great Palace in Constantinople, opposite the Church of Holy Wisdom

Cemetery of Pelagios – cemetery outside the walls of Constantinople where they throw the bodies of criminals

Chalkidon – (Chalcedon) city on the Propontis Sea opposite Constantinople

clamys – triangular cloak worn over one shoulder and fastened with a broach.

Church of the Virgin of the Copper Market – church in Constantinople that had the belt of the Virgin Mary.

Church of Holy Apostles – large church in Constantinople with the tombs of the emperors

Convent of the Mother of God on Prinkypos – convent on Prinkypos Island which Empress Irini of Athens had converted from a monastery and where she went on retreat

Kinammomon – the ancient Greek and Byzantine word for cinnamon

codex – book that came after scrolls (pl. codices)

Dalmatiou Prison – a prison in Constantinople

Daphne Palace – residence of the imperial family inside the Great Palace

Despina – title of respect for women

Diapompefsi – a public humiliation consisting of putting the victim naked backwards on a donkey and driven through the streets

Dorylaion – old Roman fortified city and military base

Ekloga – book of laws that governed the Empire of the Romans written by Emperor Leon the Isaurian

ekonomis – nun second in authority in a convent after the abbess

evkrata – a drink made from early sour apples

Evdomon – (Hebdomon) Military base seven miles outside Constantinople

follis – a copper coin (pl. folles)

forum – a large square or oval space in a Roman city with statues, fountains, or important buildings; (pl. fora)

garum – fish sauce

gerokomia – old people's homes

Hall of Nineteen Couches – a vast reception hall inside the Great Palace

haristikaris – the manager of a convent

heteria – prostitutes (pl)

Hippodrome – arena in Constantinople for chariot racing

hiremporia – pork vendor

hypourgia – nurse, pl.

ikthyopratia – fish store

inopios – wine vendor

Kallipolis – (Gallipoli), town at the mouth of the Dardanelles, on the Sea of Marmara

kandilli – candelabra

kapelarion – a family restaurant

kapelarios – owner or waiter in a kapelarion

kathisma – the covered stand in the Hippodrome for the emperor and his family

kitron – similar to a lemon

koukla – little doll (term of affection)

kouritzaki – my little girl (term of affection)

krasopatera – wino monk (a curse)

kithara – stringed instrument, similar to a guitar

Lycus River – river that flows through Constantinople

lyre – like a hand-held harp

maforion – the head scarf of a nun (pl. maforia)

magerissa – nun in a convent who manages the kitchen and shops for provisions

magirio – bread bakery

makelarion – lamb and mutton vendor

Malagina – stud farm where horses were raised for the imperial army

malakismeni – a foul curse (wanker)

Magnavra Palace – Palace inside the Great Palace where the emperor receives visitors

Master Builder – a professional builder and architect at the top of his field

milaresion – a silver coin (pl. milaresia)

mizoteris – a paid housekeeper

Nakoleia – old Roman fortress and market town

Nicaea – walled city in Bithynia where the Ecumenical Councils were held

Nikomidia – busy market city in Bithynia

omorfia mou – my pretty girl (term of affection)

oxygala – a sour milk cheese similar to yogurt

pandoheus – innkeeper

pandohion – inn

pandokissa – innkeeper's wife

patrikios – high level position appointed by the emperor

paximadia – dried bread rusks that are softened with liquid

Pelagios Cemetery – Cemetery outside the walls of Constantinople where the bodies of executed criminals were thrown into an open pit

Pelekitis Monastery – monastery in Bithynia near Constantinople

Pendykion – military fortress and town on the Propontis Sea

Piraeas – port city for Athens

plateia – an open area among the houses in a village where people gather

polykandillon – a hanging flat chandelier with glass holders for oil inserted into holes

pornovoskos – a man who buys girls from their fathers for prostitution

protarch – doctor who is chief of staff of a hospital

proyevma – breakfast

Propontis Sea – now called the Sea of Marmara

Prussa hot springs – hot mineral baths across the Propontis from Constantinople

Pontus Sea – now called the Black Sea

raptaina – seamstress

Saint's Eortologion – a yearly calendar listing the saints' days

Sampson Hospital – a large public hospital behind the Church of Holy Wisdom in Constantinople

Seflukia – port on the Roman Sea for Antioch

skaramangion – long, sleeveless garment worn over a tunica

skatopsychi – a foul curse

stratiotis – wife of a soldier

Studios Monastery – large monastery in Constantinople

Syke – port on the Roman Sea (Mediterranean) near the border to the Caliphate

szingi – fritters

Tagmata – Emperor Constantine's personal guard

theme – area of the empire similar to a province governed by a military commander

thymelikia – dancers

tonsure – the shaved part on a monk's head

trahana – a mixture of a grain and dried milk used to thicken soups and stews

valanissa – attendant in a public bathhouse

Veil of the Virgin – a scarf at Blachernae Palace said to have belonged to the Virgin Mary

verjuice – a drink made from unripe grapes

xenodohos – the admitting clerk in a hospital

zamnykistria – a sambucca player

Explore the Empress Irini Series

Book 1
Betrothal & Betrayal
Seventeen-year-old Thekla needs her quick wits and knife to track down her betrothed, a soldier who has left her at the altar for the third time. Elias the monk travels with her to Constantinople where she meets Irini of Athens, an extraordinarily beautiful orphan her same age who has been brought by powerful Emperor Constantine to marry his son, Co-emperor Leon. The two women join forces to survive this vigorous capital of the Roman Empire of the East which is rocked by religious and political strife. But will Thekla help the ambitious and ruthless Irini of Athens find the power that she craves?

Book 2
Poison is a Woman's Weapon
Irini's conniving mother-in-law, her five jealous step-brothers, and her own husband threaten Irini's safety in Constantinople. She summons Abbess Thekla, her knife-wielding friend, to bring her sharp wits and courage to get Irini safely through childbirth in the Great Palace. Thekla owes Irini her life and thus her loyalty but she is staggered by Irini's powerful ambitions which far exceed being docile wife and mother. Can Thekla survive Irini's vengeful nature and the bloody aftermath of Irini's ruthless ambition?

Book 3
Seizing Power
Constantine's father, Co-emperor Leon, dies unexpect-
edly, making Constantine emperor at age nine with Irini
as Empress Regent. Abbess Thekla's loyalty to Irini shifts
to Constantine as she watches Irini block his authority
and keep the power herself. Irini makes Constantine
wed the disliked Maria, prevents the Senate from naming
him Emperor in his own right at age 18, and imprisons
him when he tries to stop her henchmen from amassing
wealth and power. Constantine's army friends free him,
arrest her, and raise him to the throne. Resourceful as
ever, Irini will not be thwarted. Can Thekla prevent
them from murdering each other?

Book 4
The Price of Eyes
In the final book, Irini returns to the throne. She tricks
Constantine into divorcing Maria and exiles her and
Constantine's two daughters to Abbess Thekla's island
convent where Maria goes mad. Irini misleads Constan-
tine into taking revenge on the soldiers who arrested her
and the empire erupts into civil war, army against army,
Irini against Constantine. Fearing for her life, Irini traps
Constantine, wounding his eyes, but Thekla rescues him.
Irini is finally empress in her own right. But will Thekla
help her hold the throne?

Janet McGiffin lives in Manhattan and Washington State. She can be reached through her website at https://janmcgiffin.com/, https://janetmcgiffin.com/, or janmcgiffin.com